Date Due

WHITE LIGHTS ROAR

WHITE LIGHTS ROAR

A Western Story

TIM CHAMPLIN

Five Star • Waterville, Maine

First Edition
First Printing: October 2003

Published in 2003 in conjunction with
Golden West Literary Agency.

Set in 11 pt. Plantin.

Printed in the United States on permanent paper.

Library of Congress Cataloging-in-Publication Data

Champlin, Tim, 1937–
    White lights roar : a western story / by Tim Champlin.
    —1st ed.
        p. cm.
    ISBN 0-7862-3807-0 (hc : alk. paper)
    1. Illegal arms transfers—Fiction.   2. Villa, Pancho,
1878–1923—Fiction. 3. Irish—Arizona—Fiction.
    4. Revolutionaries—Fiction. 5. Arizona—Fiction. I. Title.
PS3553.H265W47 2003
813'.54—dc21   2003052879

For my grandson
Brennan Joseph Champlin

Sweep out to darkness, triumphing in his goal,
Out of the fire, out of the little room. . . .
—There is an end appointed, O my soul!
Crimson and green the signals burn; the gloom

Is hung with steam's far-blowing livid streamers.
Lost into God, as lights in light, we fly,
Grown one with will, end-drunken huddled dreamers.
The white lights roar. The sounds of the world die
And lips and laughter are forgotten things.

from "The Night Journey" (1913)
by Rupert Brooke

Prologue

"Watch it, Colonel! They're ready to fire!" Major Lindsley warned.

A uniformed officer barked a sharp command in Spanish, and the squad of eight soldiers each dropped to one knee behind the barricade. The bolts on eight rifles slid open and closed with a metallic ratcheting, locking eight live rounds in the chambers as the barrels of the weapons were leveled on the American officers a few yards from the barbed-wire fence.

"What the hell's wrong with them?" Colonel Herbert Slocum demanded. "I just want to ask a few questions concerning the whereabouts of Pancho Villa." He turned to his subordinate. "You know their lingo, Major. Tell 'em we don't mean any harm."

But the sight of those menacing muzzles had paralyzed Lindsley's tongue and he only backed away, holding out the palms of his hands toward the Mexicans in a conciliatory gesture. He could hear the quiet ticking of the four-cylinder Model T Ford roadster behind him where the enlisted driver sat in the staff car awaiting their return.

"I think we'd best get the hell out of here, sir, and leave the questions for another day," Lindsley said, finally finding his voice.

"Shit!" the colonel hissed disgustedly.

7

As if in defiance of the rifles, he turned his back on the border gate, walked deliberately to the waiting car, and climbed into the back seat. Lindsley, without taking his eyes off the squad of soldiers, stepped over the side of the open car and slid down into the seat beside the driver. The corporal, eager to be off, adjusted the throttle lever on the steering wheel and mashed the left pedal to the floor, engaging low gear. The flivver lurched forward like a black jackrabbit. The driver crimped the wheel and the spindly, high-wheeled car leaned precariously away from the turn. Then he released the pedal. With a head-snapping jerk and a metallic squeal of protest, the car bounded into its second and highest gear, and went chugging away up the dusty road toward Columbus, New Mexico, several miles to the north.

"Damned, stupid greasers," Colonel Slocum muttered, just loud enough for Lindsley to hear. "It's no wonder they can't form a stable government. The whole history of their country has been one of conquest and violent revolution."

"The United States was started with a revolution," Lindsley reminded him, turning to prop an arm on the back of the seat.

"Not the same thing at all," Slocum replied, taking off his campaign hat and wiping his face with a handkerchief. He pulled a pair of tinted glasses from his shirt pocket and put them on. "That was a hundred and thirty years ago, and there hasn't been another. It was a one-time necessity. These people . . ."—he jerked a thumb over his shoulder at the plume of dust behind the car that hid the receding border—"stir up a revolution every few years, just to have something to do, or to keep in practice." He shook his head. "The U.S. is made up mostly of thrifty people with cool heads from northern European countries. I have a theory that the people of Mexico and South America, who are a mixture mostly of hot Spanish blood and the native Indians, just don't have the temperament to settle their differences without violence."

Lindsley thought of mentioning the American Civil War, but thought better of it.

"Too much pride and arrogance," the colonel continued. "I guess when you don't have much else, you have to hold onto your pride. Look at those god-awful gaudy uniforms they wear. There's nothing in between the self-proclaimed generals and the ragged *peónes* who fight for them."

"It's probably not a good idea to generalize," Lindsley ventured.

"Look at the mongrel races the world over and you'll see that their countries haven't progressed much beyond the Stone Age," Slocum retorted.

Lindsley started to point out that there was no pure race. The history of the world was one of mixing and "mongrelizing", including the barbarian tribes of Europe that both he and the colonel were very likely descended from. But when the colonel had the bit in his teeth, there was no reining him in, so Lindsley changed the subject. "That letter from General Funston at Fort Sam Houston didn't really tell us much," he remarked.

Slocum reached into his deep shirt pocket and pulled out a wrinkled envelope. **CONFIDENTIAL** was stamped in red across the front. He unfolded the paper.

Major Lindsley had already seen the correspondence, but listened patiently while his superior officer paraphrased it. "Funston writes 'reliable' information has been received that Villa is planning to cross the border and give himself up to American authorities. Then he says that 'unreliable' information was received that Villa plans to raid American towns along the border." He folded the letter and shoved it back into his pocket. "Then, I've had reports that he was at Palomas, just across the border here, that he's on the Casas Grandes River, forty-five miles southwest of here, and that he's at Rancho Nogales, almost sixty-five miles southwest of here. What kind of sense am I to make of all that? How to sort out the rumors from the truth?"

"Well, sir, if you ask me, I think the two Mexicans who said they were attacked by *Villistas* while driving cattle some fifteen miles below the border were about as truthful as any reports you're likely to get."

"Why do you say that?"

"Those men came in voluntarily, and they were scared."

The car lurched into a rut and Colonel Slocum was thrown to one side.

"Take it easy!" he snapped at the driver. "We're in no hurry."

The car slowed as it approached the town of Columbus, and then turned off to enter the grounds of Camp Furlong.

"Too bad we have to play the game according to the rules of the politicians," Slocum said. "If we could just send a mounted patrol over the line, we could pinpoint his location in a couple of days. We wouldn't have all this guesswork."

"I think you've taken all reasonable precautions, sir," Lindsley said, recalling that the colonel had hired one of the Mexican herders, Antonio Muñoz, to go back across the border with a rifle and field glasses to see if he could locate Villa. Muñoz had returned from his one-man scout at sundown, and Lindsley had taken him in the Ford to Slocum to report. Lindsley had translated the Mexican's description of how he had found Boca Grande deserted. Villa's gang had left about three o'clock that morning, March 8th, as Muñoz had found the ashes in the campfire still warm. Through the field glasses, from a high point near the Vado de Fusiles, the old man had seen three mounted men on the road down the river towards Guzman. He said he believed about one hundred and twenty of Villa's men had ridden toward Palomas, then turned south and east, away from the border. Slocum had paid Muñoz $20 and dismissed him.

Lindsley, at the moment, was glad he was not wearing the colonel's puttees. He did not envy Slocum's burden of deciding what to believe and how to react. Lindsley had only to return to his detachment of the 13th Cavalry stationed at Gibson's Ranch, thirteen miles west of Columbus, and await orders.

The Model T pulled up to the bare, wooden headquarters building and the two men got out. At the door, Colonel Slocum stopped and faced Lindsley. "Major, I've got the responsibility of protecting sixty-five miles of vacant border, from Noría in the east to Hermanas in the west. I have to make an uninformed decision where to deploy the men I have. Just on a hunch, I'm going to beef up your outpost a little. You'll have a total of seven officers, and one hundred and fifty-one riflemen. I'll send one troop . . . two officers and sixty-five riflemen . . . to the border gate where we just came from. That will leave Columbus protected by seven officers and three hundred and forty-one men, including the headquarters and machine-gun troops. We've got women, children, and other non-combatants to think about protecting here."

"Very good, sir." Lindsley turned toward the waiting Ford. Then he stopped. "Colonel, do you think Villa would have the audacity to attack the United States? I mean, he may be an illiterate bandit, but he's cunning, they say. Surely he realizes it would bring down the whole

11

wrath of this nation on his head."

The colonel took off his tinted glasses and rubbed his dust-reddened eyes. "Major," he replied wearily, "if I knew the answer to that question, my name would be Solomon, not Slocum."

Chapter One

February, 1916
Southwestern Ireland

Tommy Glasheen had just received his eviction notice. A mounted courier had ridden up yesterday morning with the order as Glasheen was stepping out of the stone cottage to leave for his laborer's job on a Kerry County road crew.

"It's off the land by the end of the week," the courier had said. "Here's your official notice, in case you can read," he added, handing down a folded sheet of paper.

Had he not been so stunned by the suddenness of it all, Glasheen would have yanked the young whelp out of his saddle and beaten the snot out of him for his impudence. Instead, he only took the paper, his mind in a whirl. "I've paid m'rent on time," was all he could think to say.

"This is not about rent," the young rider said. "Lord Grisham has need of the land for grazing his sheep."

"But we've lived here twenty-two years!" Glasheen protested, taking his wife's arm as she stepped out the door into the early rays of the sun to see who the visitor could be.

"You think this is your land because you've lived here all that time? This is Lord Grisham's land and he has other uses for it, that's all I know. So it's out of here by Sunday next or the place will be pulled down about your ears." He tugged his horse's head around to ride off, but then seemed to soften a bit and looked back over his shoulder. "Lord Grisham has nothing against you. Parliament passed some change in the tax laws that will penalize him for keeping so many tenants. He'll do much better grazing sheep." The young courier kicked his horse and galloped away.

Gazing after him, Glasheen had the odd thought that the sleek, black gelding the man rode was probably worth more than all he and his wife owned after decades of toil. He looked at her, and the hurt in her brown eyes was almost more than he could bear. He pulled her close so she wouldn't see his own tears forming. "Ann, Ann, it'll be all right. You'll see," he said huskily, stroking her hair. He could feel her silently sobbing against his shoulder.

It was now thirty-six hours later and the shock and rage had subsided into a burning in the pit of his stomach. In spite of the fact that he needed his low-paying job more than ever now, he'd told the foreman that he was ill and had left work just after noon today. He'd gone home and told Ann he wanted to lie down for a short nap, and then he was going to Riordan's Tavern for a special meeting.

"I've been holding back my support, but now's the time for action," he told her. "I thought maybe we could get by, minding our own business and working hard, instead of joining those hotheads who are always talking revolution." He heaved a great sigh as he sat down on the bed to pull off his heavy brogans. "But the English bulldog just keeps biting. It's time to act. I have no choice now."

"Will you be wantin' some supper then, before ya go?"

"Don't bother about me. I'll get a bowl of Riordan's good mutton stew."

"Who will be at the meetin', then?" she asked.

"Men from every faction, I expect," he replied. "The Citizens' Army, Home Rule, the Agrarians, some against the war, some for the war, those against conscription. But the loudest will be Rory Donahue, who gets his orders directly from Pearse and the other leaders in Dublin who've decided to strike for complete independence. They're planning some kind of armed uprising."

"If that happens, when will it be? And will all the people rise up and join in?"

He stretched his stocky body out on the bed with a groan. "Ah, Ann, you've hit on the two biggest questions. The first one, we can decide . . . the second, no one but the good Lord and two million Irishmen know the answer to."

Two hours later Glasheen was striding down the deserted road towards Riordan's, two miles away. He pulled his wool cap lower to shield his eyes against the cold February mist blowing in off the Atlantic, and hunched his shoulders down in his threadbare jacket. He'd get to the tavern early—time for supper and a quiet pint or two before the others showed up and all the fiery talk and arguing started. Not a joiner by nature, he hoped all the talk would lead to something positive. It had to be soon. His wife could go to her sister's place in Killarney for a short time, but he was now itching for action, born of frustration.

At the time of his birth, in 1864, the Great Hunger was still a searing agony to most adults. Although he had no memory of doing so, he must have been weaned directly from his mother's milk to a hatred of the British—a bitter sustenance he'd been chewing on ever since. Lacking any formal education beyond the age of fourteen, he'd been schooled in subservient toil. He and Ann had married in their twenties and had reared four children to adulthood. They had scrambled for every scrap of food and clothing. Ann had lost their second son in infancy to scarlet fever that carried the baby off within a week. Even if they could have afforded a doctor, it was unlikely the child could have been saved. In after years this was some consolation, but the pain of loss at the time had been like an abscessed tooth. By working long hours and taking any job available, by raising a few sheep and pigs and potatoes, he and Ann had somehow gotten through those early years of marriage and child-bearing without once going on the dole. It was a source of pride for them that they'd managed to do for themselves with little outside help from the parish or friends.

At one time, when he was still single, he'd considered moving to Dublin and taking a job for wages. But he hated crowded cities. If he were destined to live on the edge of poverty all his life, he'd much prefer to do it in the open air of County Kerry. On the same trip, he'd traveled on to London with two companions who were out seeking their fortunes. Used to the slow pace of the countryside in the rugged west of Ireland, he'd been appalled at the crowds, the noise, and the stench of the city where a pint of Guinness and a hotel room were so dear he'd quit drinking and, for a week, slept in the park, but to no avail, since his money had been stolen by a pickpocket anyway.

But all of that was past now. It was a happy faculty of the human mind that painful memories were usually sup-pressed, while the happy times were retained. The good events, the funny stories, family gatherings—things that, along with an adequate supply of poteen or Guinness, glad-dened the heart.

Now, as he swung along the uphill incline, his mind was on nothing more profound than a warm turf fire and a bowl of hot stew. At the top of the grade, he slowed down, his heart thumping strongly in his chest. He'd been walking too fast. No need to hurry. He paused for a moment and looked back down the gently rising road of crushed stone. It was a road he himself had helped repair several weeks before. It's not as if there was much traffic hereabouts to damage the roads. Motorcars and lorries had become common in most places, but men like himself could never afford one. A donkey and a jaunting cart still sufficed for their few travel needs. Starvation and emigration during the great famine seventy years before had cut Ireland's population by more than half, and County Kerry was still one of the poorest, least populated counties in the country. But no problems of man could detract from the physical beauty of the place, he reflected.

As the sun dropped toward the western sea to be extinguished for the night, it came out from under the layer of dark clouds. Slanting rays of light picked up the gray-green waves rolling up the long inlet. Each successive wave surged against a jutting pile of black boulders, the powerful ridge of water shattering and exploding high into the air in a lather of foam. Even with a strong westerly blowing, he could not hear the crashing of the surf from this distance. Those waves had come rolling and pounding into that long cove for hundreds, or perhaps thousands, of years. But his was a mind not given much to speculation. He dealt with the here and now, never having the leisure or inclination to tackle philosophy, or what might have been in ancient times, or—beyond the rules of the Church—God's relationship to man.

He turned and resumed his walking, noting the sunlight on the hillside to his right. The deep, waving grass was a beautiful sight, all right, and was one of several shades of green that led tourists, long ago, to dub this the Emerald Isle. But, to his practical eye, this was a particular type of grass that contained little nutrition for grazing livestock.

The road curved around the base of the treeless hill and

Riordan's Tavern came into view. It was a low structure with a thin wisp of smoke streaming sideways from its chimney. The squat building had been there for as long as he could remember—several generations, the old ones said. It seemed as solid as the rocks from which it was constructed, as permanent as the castle and monastery ruins that pre-dated the Viking raids. But, to Glasheen, as to many others of the region, it was a second home, and it's proprietor, Joseph Riordan, a second father confessor.

"Ah, Joe," Glasheen said, forcing the door open against a gust and letting it slam and latch behind him. At five-foot, six inches, he didn't even have to duck to keep from knocking his head on the lintel. "A bowl o' your famous stew and a pint, if ya please." He dropped his cap on a table near the window and wiped the sheen of moisture from his face with the other hand.

The lean man behind the bar nodded without speaking. To a stranger, Riordan with the solemn face, the slicked-down black hair, and the heavy brows might seem a taciturn man. But Glasheen had come to know him as a gentle soul who invited confidences by his ability to listen, to sympathize, and to keep his own counsel. With only a word or two of consolation, the bartender usually topped off his attention with a foaming glass of stout that he'd been drawing while some anguished customer was pouring out his troubles.

"Howling like a banshee out there," Riordan remarked, setting down a bowl of steaming mutton stew and pint of dark Guinness in front of Glasheen. "A time or two in the past hour, I thought it might lift m'roof off."

"Not likely, Joe." Glasheen chuckled. "You wove that thatch yourself, didn't you?"

The bartender nodded. "Me and m'two sons. It's been

18

there these eighteen months past."

"Then I know we're safe for the day," he said, laying down three coins to pay for the food and drink. With no change of expression, Riordan took the money and moved away.

As Glasheen ate, he listened to the wind howling around the eaves. The Atlantic gales and rain that swept in much of the year might be a nuisance, but they also helped bring the Gulf Stream that kept their northerly island free of the snow and bitter winters that Norway got.

He took a long pull at the foamy glass of stout and relaxed, allowing the peace of the place to seep into him. He had never analyzed the effect this pub had on him. Maybe it was the familiar things—the same two old farmers playing dominoes and smoking their long-stemmed meerschaum pipes, a pint each, and a half dozen words stretching out to fill their whole afternoon. Glasheen chewed thoughtfully, aware of the aromatic pipe smoke and unique, almost sweetish smell of the turf fire in the grate.

By the time he'd wiped up the last of the stew with the last crust of brown bread, several men had begun to drift in. There was James King, Sean McDevitt, William Leary, Rory Donahue, and three or four others Glasheen recognized by face, if not readily by name—men who had traveled several miles by horse or motorcar to be here—men who were the organizers or captains of the volunteer companies of citizen-soldiers in the neighboring counties. It had been their habit to gather here once every fortnight or so to co-ordinate their activities. They exchanged news of the Great War on the continent, and whether England was distracted and weakened enough by it for the downtrodden Irish finally to break free. Riordan's was chosen as the meeting place because of its remote location. Any stranger would be instantly recognized

19

and ejected. There was only a remote possibility that any hostile ears might hear and report their plans to the British authorities. But it wasn't as if those politicians didn't know the whole island was fomenting revolution. It had been British policy to be conciliatory here, firm there, and try to fragment the Irish into as many inept factions as possible.

Headlights shone briefly through the window as a truck pulled up out front. The two ancient domino players looked up irritably, then nodded to each other and swept the ivory pieces off the table, preparing to leave.

The door opened and closed as the driver of the truck entered and headed straight for the bar.

Riordan looked up from dropping some coins into the cash drawer. "What's your pleasure?"

"I've got a thirst you couldn't cut with a cleaver," the man said. "A pint of bitters and keep 'em comin' until I tell ya to stop."

There was a hubbub of voices, punctuated by hearty laughter among the men who apparently hadn't seen each other for some time. Riordan was busy filling shot glasses and drawing pints.

Two or three of the men nodded to Glasheen who remained sitting by himself near the window. Rory Donahue gave the men only about five minutes to socialize and settle in with their drinks before he rapped on the table with a blackthorn walking stick. Glasheen was of the opinion that Donahue always carried the stick more as a symbol of his self-importance than anything else.

"Let's get down to business! Some of us have come a good distance."

The voices in the room gradually subsided. The burly truck driver was apparently sharing a joke with a man at the bar and had his back to Donahue. They continued talking, and then burst out laughing at the punch line.

"Hold it down, Mike, we've got business here!"

The truck driver turned around and regarded the slender Donahue. "And sure it's a serious man we've got for our leader," he commented dryly.

There was a general chuckle as Donahue's face flushed slightly in the lamplight.

"It's a damned good thing somebody takes these things seriously," he replied evenly, "or our grandsons would be standin' here a hundred years from now still drinking and complaining of the English."

A thin smile creased the beefy face of the truck driver who put his hands up, palms out, in sign of mock surrender. "Carry on, m'lad."

Rory Donahue stood with one foot on a chair and looked around at the men seated in a semi-circle and leaning against the bar, facing him. He said nothing for several seconds until the room was so quiet Glasheen could hear the creaking of the sign hanging over the door outside. The man should have been an actor, Glasheen thought.

"I got word yesterday from the men in Dublin," Donahue finally began, referring to the leaders. "They've set the date. It will commence on Easter weekend . . . sometime between Friday and Monday."

"What will?" King asked.

"The rising, of course! What do ye think been discussin' here these past months? It will start under the guise of weekend military maneuvers, so the British won't realize it's the real thing, until it's too late."

"That time's not very precise," Leary said.

"We'll get word in plenty of time," Donahue assured him. "It's only February. Our job is to be ready. Now, let me get a report from each of ye, starting with ye, Leary."

Glasheen listened with only half an ear as Donahue went around the room, getting verbal reports from the men as to the state of readiness of their various volunteer companies. What he did hear was not encouraging—men who couldn't attend drill because of work, men marching and having mock battles with wooden guns, understrength companies due to lack of volunteers.

"The wives and women of Galway will furnish us with pigs and cabbages and carrots," one of the men said. "We've got all the support we could ask for in our county."

"Our men have already got home-baked bread and quilts while we were trainin'," another added. "And we didn't even have to ask for 'em. The families in our district are all behind us."

Glasheen wanted to raise his hand and ask Donahue if this sounded like a populace who could rise up and crush the British army, or defend themselves against being crushed in retaliation. But he held his silence. To a man, all of those here were younger than he and just naturally full of hellfire and hatred. He would be scoffed at for being old and conservative.

"I reported to you last time about the Irish Brigade that's now being trained in Germany by German officers. They're ready to cross the channel and strike when Pearse gives the word."

"What about arms?" McDevitt asked. "We've got to have something to fight with besides some outmoded guns with all different calibers and very little ammunition."

"We've been in negotiations with the German government through their embassy in New York for about two years," Donahue said. "They've agreed to supply us with twenty thousand rifles and a good supply of ammunition. They'll disguise a ship to look like a Norwegian freighter and rendezvous with our men at a designated point and time on the west coast on Good Friday. The details are still secret, but the guns will be off-loaded and distributed by rail up and down the west coast so our companies of volunteers can all act in unison as soon as we get word from Dublin that the uprising has begun."

"Trusting the Huns is like letting a wolf pack into your sheep pasture," King remarked. "Before it's over we'll be saluting the Kaiser and digging potatoes for Berlin's green grocers."

Donahue turned a cold eye on the speaker. "Who's been your worst enemy these three centuries past . . . the Germans or the British? The Germans are supplying weapons so we can help weaken England for them. The war on the western front is stalemated in the trenches. The Germans are desperate to get any advantage they can. They're afraid America will enter the war and turn the balance against them."

"Can the Germans be trusted to come through on their delivery?" King persisted.

"Well, we have their assurance, and it's certainly in their best interest. They've even offered to supply some German officers to lead our civilian soldiers." He shook his head. "Frankly, I don't think that's a good idea, and I've told the men in Dublin so. Generally, the Huns are too strict for a bunch of civilians who aren't used to disciplined military ways."

"Maybe that's what our volunteer army needs," McDevitt said.

"No. If we were going to be led by German officers, they should have been here all along so we could get used to them."

"At least the British haven't passed a conscription law

and haven't tried to disarm our volunteers," another man said.

"That's like a dog being grateful his master kicks him only three times a day instead of five," Donahue sneered. "What is it, Sweeney?" Donahue pointed at a man who had raised his hand to speak.

"I'm representing Sinn Fein, as you know," he began. "We are very much against an armed insurrection."

"And may I be askin' why?" Donahue glanced around the room as if to see what others were going to join in his ridicule. "The very meaning of the name suggests 'ourselves alone'. . . self-reliance."

"The members of our organization are very much in favor of independence," Sweeney continued. "We just don't think a direct attack is the way to achieve it. The IRB . . . Irish Revolutionary Brotherhood, which has recently been reorganized as the Irish Republican Brotherhood . . . tried an armed uprising in Eighteen Sixty-Seven and failed. . . ."

"But it had great influence in encouraging Parnell to become militant in Parliament," Donahue broke in, "and it gave a big push to the Land League struggles that followed. Even Pearse became a member of the IRB three years ago."

"Let me finish," Sweeney continued patiently. "Sinn Fein believes that guerrilla warfare is the way to eventually win our independence . . . not a straight-up battle with a superior, trained army."

"The men in Dublin are afraid the war might end before we can take advantage of our opportunity and hit the British when they're not looking," Donahue said.

"There's a rumor that even Roger Casement wants to postpone this uprising, unless we can get German troops to join it."

"If you listen to every rumor . . . ," Donahue sneered.

"Dammit! Wait a minute!" Sweeney exploded, red-faced. "Hear me out. Isn't that what this meeting is for?" Silence fell.

"OK, as I started to say, we haven't learned our lessons from history. Remember John Brown in Eighteen Fifty-Nine, just before the start of the American Civil War? He was so sure the slaves in the South would rise up and join him to fight for their freedom that he and a few of his followers attacked the federal arsenal at Harper's Ferry, Virginia to supply some of them with guns. The slaves did not rise up. John Brown and his boys were caught and hanged. Mark my words, the same thing could happen here." Sweeney finished speaking and sat down abruptly.

Donahue let the silence hang in the air for a few seconds. "All right, then. You've gone on record as saying Sinn Fein opposes the uprising. I'm sure the men in Dublin have considered guerrilla warfare as an alternative, and have rejected it as a strategy. It would take us another two hundred years to throw off the British with only hit-and-run tactics. In any case, the decision has been made. You're either in or you're out, but the uprising is going forward. It's too late to stop it."

"If anything goes wrong, do we have a backup plan?" McDevitt asked. "I think this whole idea is bad. Too much left to chance. Trusting people we don't know."

"There's one mission that could give us another load of rifles in case the Germans default at the last minute." Donahue stood up straighter and let one of his famous pregnant pauses fill the room. All eyes were on him. "We have a lead on a shipment of about four thousand Krag-Jorgenson rifles with ammunition in America that are available, if we hurry. I can't give you the details right now, but we need to select one man to go to the States, contact the individual who has them, negotiate their sale and delivery to us . . . and we must do it quickly. We have only two months." He looked around. "Does anyone here wish to volunteer?"

Silence. The men turned and looked at each other.

"I have a man in mind who would be perfect for this job," Donahue continued. He turned and pointed dramatically at Tommy Glasheen. There was a stir in the room, and Glasheen felt his throat constrict.

"What do ye say, Tommy?" Donahue asked. "Will ye go f'the sake of us all?"

"Give me a rifle. I'd rather stay here and fight," Glasheen managed to reply, clearing his throat.

"No offense, Tommy, but ye couldn't hit the turf with your face if you'd taken aboard a keg o' Guinness," the beefy truck driver growled. A laugh rippled around the room.

"The British bastards just evicted me and Ann," Glasheen said, feeling himself being swept into volunteering for something he had no wish to do.

"I heard. That's why I'm askin'. Some o' your fellows here in Kerry were evicted by the same landlord, but they all have young folk at home or are carin' for elderly parents. We can see to Ann's well-being while you're gone a month or so. Your expenses will be paid."

This shot down the next argument Glasheen was about to voice.

"I've never been over the water," he managed to say.

"Riordan, refill this man's glass! He sounds as if he has a frog in his throat," Donahue called. Then, to Glasheen: "Why, man, several of us talked it over earlier, and you'd be the ideal one to go. You're diplomatic, you've got a glib tongue, and, most of all, you're as tenacious as a bulldog. Ye know how to get things done in spite of any setbacks. I only know ye by reputation, but I'm told your reputation is well deserved. You're as solid as a rock who's weathered many a storm."

If he only knew how much of that was due to luck, Glasheen thought.

"You could do more for the cause of Irish liberty by saying yes, than if you were leading a whole brigade of troops, because you can secure the guns that can arm those troops."

Glasheen knew he was trapped. He swallowed hard and looked about at the expectant faces. He knew he was being set up and shamelessly flattered, but he also knew he couldn't very well decline now, without looking like a complete coward. In any case, while Donahue had been going on, Glasheen had had a little time to reconsider. And suddenly it seemed like an adventure. Whether or not he secured the guns, it would be a great opportunity for a trip abroad, possibly the adventure of a lifetime. All his life he'd been a drudge. Now was his chance to break out. He accepted the full, foaming glass Riordan handed him, took a swallow, and set it down. "I'll do it!"

The roar of a cheer nearly lifted the thatched roof off Riordan's tavern.

Chapter Two

The biplane dropped suddenly and James Whitlaw gasped as his stomach seemed to catch in his throat. He instinctively gripped the padded cowling of the cockpit. Stiffened legs thrust him back in his seat, away from the onrushing ground, as the aircraft continued to fall beneath him. In only a few seconds—that seemed like forever—the fabric of the wings flexed slightly and Whitlaw felt their descent slow as the biplane was gently buoyed up on a rising thermal from the desert below.

He swallowed hard, his heart pounding, embarrassed that he still hadn't gotten used to these rolling currents of air. It was just like riding a boat on a surging sea. Man was out of his element in both places, he reflected; the only difference here was the instinctive human fear of falling. Licking lips that were dry from the blast of the slipstream, he wondered if he just didn't have the feel for flying. Lieutenant Wilford Scoggins was giving him free lessons, and Whitlaw was determined to stick to it until he soloed. Whitlaw had hinted a time or two that he was ready to take the Jenny up alone, but Scoggins had demurred with the remark: "You need a little more time up there with me in the back seat, before I turn you loose. It can get tricky, and I want you to be comfortable in any situation."

Just now he'd felt his eyes go wide and the blood drain

from his face and knew that Scoggins was right. He dared not look around at his instructor who was piloting the plane from the rear cockpit for fear his own face would betray him.

This March afternoon they'd flown west, as usual, along the railroad tracks that paralleled the Mexican border. From three thousand feet up, the shiny rails looked like one heavy black line drawn straight across the dun-colored desert floor. Following these tracks was about the only sure way to fly a straight course. Colonel Slocum, crusty commanding officer of Camp Furlong, had warned Lieutenant Scoggins in blunt terms to make sure he stayed on the United States side of the border. "We don't want you crashing that contraption on the Mexican side and causing some international incident with those damned rebels. The way things have been going lately, Villa and his boys would just love an excuse to start something."

"The colonel isn't saying *if* I crash, he's saying *when* I crash," Scoggins had remarked to Whitlaw later when they were alone. "He's of the old school. Coming up on his sixty-first birthday, and thinks the military should never change. No faith in the future of flying machines." Whitlaw noticed Scoggins eyeing his graying hair and lean, lined face. Then the lieutenant added, almost as an afterthought: "No offense. I know you're older than the colonel, but you've got a younger, more flexible mind."

Whitlaw recalled this exchange as his eyes followed the tracks to where they disappeared into the haze on the flat horizon. Navigation was not the problem now, he reflected. He was more concerned with getting the feel of the wheel and the pedals and controlling the craft in unpredictable winds. He was proud of the way he'd handled the controls early in the flight today, keeping the craft steady in a quartering wind. It was getting a little easier. When he'd first started, the boxy airplane had seemed awkward and unwieldy. He'd been an athlete in his youth and still retained good hand/eye co-ordination. But, initially, operating the wheel and the pedals had been like riding a unicycle and bouncing a basketball at the same time.

Now they had come in sight of the low desert mountain that was their landmark and Scoggins had taken over, preparing to bank around for the ten minute flight back to Columbus, New Mexico.

The pilot nosed the Jenny down and Whitlaw squinted through his goggles at the sun flashing on the blur of the varnished propeller. Unless there was a change in the pitch, he was nearly unaware of the roar of the engine once they were aloft. Then they were into their easy bank and he looked over the side of the cockpit at the mesquite and sage that dotted the desert floor far below. *Maybe I was born too soon,* he thought. He knew, at age sixty-four, he probably wouldn't live long enough to see the airplane developed into a safe, routine way of travel. Not that he could imagine aviation ever becoming so safe that it would be boring. He recalled the thrill of his first airplane ride at a county fair in Iowa in 1914, only two years ago. After they were safely back on the grassy field and his knees had stopped trembling, he could hardly get his money out fast enough to buy another ticket. Being free of the earth and able to see the land and trees and rivers for miles around, to feel the wind whipping his hair, and hear the air humming through the wires and struts had made him feel like the ruler of the universe—an expansion of his being. To be above it all was to be master of it all. The fear and the exaltation were intertwined. Now, two years and many flights later, little had changed. But fear was a good thing, if controlled. It engendered caution and attention to detail—habits that might someday keep him alive in this dangerous pursuit.

With these musings, it seemed hardly any time before the cluster of box-like buildings of Columbus came into view ahead. Just southeast of town, Whitlaw picked out the colorful windsock held stiff by a southerly breeze. Windless days here were rare, he reflected, as Scoggins circled the drill field and lined up his landing into the wind. Landings were the most difficult part of flying, Whitlaw had discovered. Anything could happen—a sudden gust of wind could dip a wing and cause a ground loop, a wheel could hit an unseen hole. He held his breath as they dropped the last few feet and the ground came rushing up to meet them. The wheels touched and bounced once, twice, then they were down and rolling. A hundred yards on the packed dirt and dry grass brought them to a big hangar—actually an unused stable that Lieutenant Scoggins had acquired the use of.

"Get the doors!" Scoggins yelled above the idling engine.

Whitlaw unbuckled his lap belt and climbed stiffly over the side of the cockpit, stepping carefully onto the fragile wing, and down. He unlatched and swung the big doors wide, bracing them open as Scoggins cut the switch and the propeller spun to a halt. Small sounds became suddenly audible in the silence—a bird chirping in a big mesquite bush a few yards away, the wind rattling small pebbles against the wooden hangar.

The two men usually flew just after sunup to avoid the wind that was created by the build-up of heat later in the day. They pushed the plane into the hangar, and swung the doors shut. Scoggins never left the aircraft outside. The Curtiss JN-2 was his pride and joy since he'd purchased it from a civilian in El Paso who'd crash-landed it. The damage was not severe, except to the psyche of the pilot, so the price was low. Scoggins, who'd always wanted to fly, hired a mechanic and the two of them repaired the plane. Then he'd paid an Army pilot to teach him to fly in his off hours, and now he was taking on the rôle of instructor for Whitlaw, a retired railroad man.

"You got time for a beer and some lunch?" Scoggins asked as the two men walked toward the mess shacks.

"I've got nothing but time." Whitlaw grinned. "You're the one who's got to fit all this in with active duty."

The younger man shrugged. "It's just a good thing I'm doing this flying on my own, so the old man has nothing official to say about it. You can bet I'd be grounded or court-martialed if I was flying on government time. Although, technically, an officer belongs to the Army twenty-four hours a day." He grinned. "Sometimes Colonel Slocum looks right through me like I'm a ghost. I'm sure he expects me to be killed in a crash before long, and he's already wondering who he'll get as a replacement."

Whitlaw chuckled. "Come on. As long as you're still alive, let's walk up to the hotel and I'll buy you lunch."

"You don't need to do that."

"I want to. We've eaten at your house the last two times, and I don't feel comfortable eating on post as your guest since I'm not in the military. Besides," he added, glancing at Scoggins's jodhpurs and riding boots, "you're on leave today. No sense hanging around the post."

"You're on, then. Let's go." Scoggins stuffed the leather helmet and goggles into his jacket pocket and hurried to keep pace with Whitlaw's longer stride.

The two men walked north, up the dirt street, and crossed the railroad track that ran east and west and bisected the hamlet of barely three hundred people. Except for the fact that Columbus was on the El Paso & Southwestern Railroad, and hosted the 13th Cavalry regiment, the town had little reason for existence. It was located on flat desert terrain, seventy-five miles west of El Paso, thirty-two miles south of Deming, and three miles north of the Mexican border. Aside from Camp Furlong, which housed nearly six hundred men, the entire town consisted of a few small stores, two hotels, a post office, a bank, and an odd collection of frame and adobe houses. With very little greenery to soften the bleak aspect of the town, it was nearly as eye-wearying as the landscape around it. The few townspeople could not afford to waste precious water on trees and shrubs, even for use as windbreaks. So the daily winds that moaned around the buildings raised clouds of dust to coat everything—adobe and frame buildings alike—a uniform brown.

To Jim Whitlaw, who had grown up in the green, undulating fields of a small town in Iowa, the hostile terrain was something he still couldn't adjust to even after living the past ten months here. But it was new and different—a complete break with the past. He'd chosen this remote place to dull the painful memory of both a dead wife and the forced retirement from his job, as well as the physical pain that wear and the advancing years were beginning to bring. It was dry here, and warm in the winter—just what his doctor had recommended for possible relief of the tendonitis in his thumbs and both shoulders, and the painful bursitis in his right arm. Whitlaw couldn't tell if it had helped much so far, but at least he was out of the snowstorms and bitter weather of the Midwest. Only his new friend, Lieutenant Wilford Scoggins—at age thirty-nine, twenty-five years his junior—had kept Whitlaw's retirement from being very boring. The flying lessons had been an unexpected bonus.

The two men reached the wooden steps to the hotel porch and stepped up into the shade. It was not a hot day—that would come in three or four months—but Whitlaw noticed that Scoggins's face was red and wind-burned where the goggles had not protected it. He rubbed a hand across his own forehead and felt the fine grit. "Wait a minute." He dug into his pants pocket for a comb and ran it through the hair that was still thick but heavily gray. "I look like a bum," he said, squinting at his pale reflection in the front window of the hotel. "Didn't even shave this morning."

"You think anyone in here is going to notice?" Scoggins said. "Or care? This isn't the Waldorf." He swept his arm at their surroundings. A tumbleweed went bounding and rolling down the street and finally lodged against the radiator of a parked Stearns touring car. Except for two pedestrians a block away, Columbus had the aspect of a ghost town.

Whitlaw grinned as he shoved the comb back into his pocket. "I may be retired, but that's no reason to let my personal appearance go to hell."

Scoggins shook his head as he led the way into the hotel dining room and found a table near a front window.

"I'll have the roast beef with potatoes, corn, lima beans, and bread . . . and a beer," Whitlaw said a few minutes later, handing the menu back to the mustachioed Mexican waiter.

"Very good, *señor*. And you?" He turned to Scoggins.

"Bacon and eggs and coffee."

The waiter nodded and departed.

Scoggins looked across the table at Whitlaw. "This is breakfast for me. I don't eat before I go up."

"Subject to air sickness?"

"Not usually, but I've felt queasy a time or two. You're eating a pretty heavy lunch," he commented. "You planning a nap this afternoon?"

"I can't nap when it's bright outside. This is my main meal of the day. I don't sleep well if I eat or drink a lot at night. Hot milk or hot cocoa about a half hour before bedtime makes me sleep better." He shook his head. "Damn! Listen to me. I sound just like my grandfather used to. It's hell to get old," he added, absently rubbing and scratching his right arm.

"That bursitis still bothering you?" Scoggins asked, noting the action.

"Nothing I can't live with," Whitlaw said. "It burns and tingles from shoulder to wrist most of the time when I'm not moving it. Feels like it's about half asleep. But it's fine when I'm using it."

The two men fell silent for a minute or two. A young couple with two small children sat nearby. Across the room two salesmen in shirtsleeves and vests were conversing earnestly over their meal. The hotel was a favorite stopover for drummers working their way from town to town by rail. The *clinking* of silverware and the hum of conversation were the only sounds in the room.

A gust of wind rattled the nearby window, and Whitlaw looked out into the nearly deserted, sunlit street. It was just a year ago tomorrow—March 9, 1915—that Jane, his wife of thirty-four years, had died of a malignant tumor the doctors were unable to cure. Toward the end, doses of pain medicine gave her some relief and made her sleep. The details of that scene were burned into his memory. He didn't even need to close his eyes to see himself sitting in a cane rocker by her bedside.

From where he sat, he could see, in the next room, the yellow and blue flames flickering behind the mica windows of a nickel-plated oil-burning stove that warmed the first floor of their frame house. Outside the bedroom window, the light was fading from a blustery March day with dark clouds and bursts of rain against the glass.

After hours of restless dreams and incoherent mutterings, she awakened long enough to take a little water. She'd swallowed two tablespoons of beef broth, murmured a barely audible—"Thank you."—before lapsing into a deep sleep. As he kept his lonely vigil, it began to grow dark in the room and he got up and lit the coal-oil lamp on the dresser, turning it low. Back at her bedside, he checked her barely perceptible breathing and pulse. The rocker creaked as he sat back down. In the quiet, he could hear the shelf clock ticking in the sitting room, and was aware of every detail around him—the hooked rug make by her mother, the pattern of the handmade quilt that had been a wedding gift, the framed tintypes of their parents on the wall, the reflection of the lamp on the polished oak floor.

The next thing he knew, he was opening his eyes. He'd dozed, and his neck was stiff. He got up to check his wife and re-alized she'd stopped breathing. There was no pulse. The hand of grief clutched at his throat. She'd slipped away as he slept. He straightened her in the bed, folding her hands on her flannel nightgown, her brown hair flaring out on the pillow. He checked her signs once again, just to be sure. Taking a deep breath, he turned away, wishing that at least one of their two grown chil-dren had been there to share his sorrow. His eyes lit on a printed card that lay on the dresser—a prayer attributed to St. Francis that he had often read and pondered these past months. He picked up the card and held it near the lamp. **Be at peace,** *it* read in part. **Do not look forward in fear to the changes in life . . . God will lead you safely through all things, and, when you cannot stand it, He will bury you in His arms. Do not fear what may happen tomorrow. The same everlasting Father who cares for you today** *will take care of you then and every day. He will either shield you from suffering or will give you unfailing strength to bear it.*

The words blurred in his vision as a sob caught in his throat.

"Jim! Jim! Are you OK?" It was the low, insistent voice of Wilford Scoggins.

Whitlaw came to himself to see his friend staring across the table at him. "Yeah, yeah." He blinked tears away and rubbed his eyes, attempting to erase the painful memory. "All this dust blowing around has got my eyes irritated something awful. Maybe I'll take to wearing my bifocals all the time to protect my eyes some."

The waiter arrived with their food at that moment, and Whitlaw was saved from making any further excuses.

"This probably isn't any of my business, but what brought you to this god-forsaken hunk of desert, anyway? The Army sent me or I'd damn' sure be some place else," Scoggins said, sopping up yellow egg yolk with a piece of bread.

"My doc thought a dry, warm climate might be good for my enflamed tendons and the bursitis."

"There are lots of warm, dry places better than this. Hell, even Yuma would be preferable, in my opinion. It rivals hell in the summer months, but at least there are more people there, and it's got a river." He shook his head as he took a bite. "And you're a good long ways from your kids and grandkids, too. Is that the reason you want to learn to fly?"

"No. That's just for fun. I'll take the train back East to see my son in Council Bluffs and daughter in Illinois. The grandkids will be out of school, then, and we'll have a good time. I don't want to wear out my welcome going too often.

I'll visit Jane's grave while I'm there, and also some of my old friends in Omaha."

The lieutenant gave him a quizzical look over the rim of his coffee mug. "I'm a pretty good judge of men," he remarked, setting down the cup. "And I'd bet a month's pay that you have another reason for living in this dusty little hamlet."

"What makes you think so?"

"You have no kin here, as far as I know. And a retired man could live anywhere he chooses. But the clincher is, as much as you like to read, there's not even a bookstore, library, or newspaper in this place. An intellectual man like yourself is not going to be satisfied reading the labels on soup cans."

Whitlaw took a long swallow of his beer and wiped his mouth with a napkin. "OK, OK. I guess if I can trust you with my life in the clouds, you can be trusted to keep what I'm about to tell you confidential," he said slowly. He glanced around to be sure they were not within earshot of anyone in the room.

Scoggins nodded his understanding.

"It's true, I came here for my health to get away from those Midwestern blizzards, but I chose this place mainly to make a stab at clearing my name." He paused to take a bite of potatoes and gravy. "I spent thirty-two years with the Union Pacific Railroad, but was forced out because my superiors suspected me of planning the disappearance of a big load of rifles and ammunition."

"Oh?"

"I started out as a section hand, rose to section boss in Missouri Valley, Iowa, then moved on to brakeman. Luckily this was after the Westinghouse air brakes and automatic couplers came into use and the job wasn't quite as hazardous as before. But I was still glad when I got promoted to conductor. Held that job for twenty years. Wish I had finished my time riding the trains. Sometimes a man can overreach himself and the results can be disastrous. A job of dispatcher came open and it paid a little more, so I applied. With my good record and the help of a close friend above me, I got it. Once I learned the job, I did OK, but one big problem came up that I was blamed for, even though I had nothing to do with it. When you hold a position of responsibility like that, you take the blame for anything in your jurisdiction that goes wrong."

"Just like the military," Scoggins agreed. "If something goes well, the higher ranking officers get the credit . . . if something screws up, the blame is pushed down to the lowest rank possible."

Whitlaw nodded, chewing a mouthful of roast beef. He swallowed and continued. "I'd been a dispatcher for about two years when the War Department declared eight thousand Krag-Jorgensen rifles government surplus and put them on the open market for civilians to buy for use as sporting rifles. That bolt action, five-shot repeater was the standard military weapon during the Spanish-American War. They used it until the Army adopted the Nineteen-Oh-Three model Springfield several years ago."

"I know," Scoggins said. "Norwegian design. The Krag was the first weapon using smokeless powder the ordnance board approved. I've fired it and the Oh-Three. For my money, there's not a nickel's worth of difference between the two, except the Krag has a smoother action. The Army went with the Springfield because it's clip-loaded, like the Mausers they faced in Cuba."

Whitlaw nodded, taking a swallow of beer. "Well, anyway, the first four thousand rifles with lots of Thirty-Forty ammunition were bought by a chain of stores on the

West Coast that were going to retail them. They were crated and shipped by rail from a government armory in the East. When they got to Omaha, they were transferred to the UP, and I dispatched them to Los Angeles via the Southern Pacific and the El Paso and Southwestern. To make a long story a little shorter, the whole train and its crew just vanished. It passed through here without stopping about ten, one night, then through Hachita, forty-five miles west of here an hour or so later. That's the last anyone saw of it. If it went through Animas in the early hours of the morning, as scheduled, no one can recall seeing it. Animas is the last little town this side of the Arizona border."

"Oh, I remember that incident!" Scoggins interrupted, his fork poised in the air. "Going on two years ago now, as I recall. Big splash in the papers about it. I was stationed in Virginia at the time."

"The whole train consisted of a locomotive, tender, two boxcars, and a caboose."

"What was it doing on the El Paso and Southwestern?" Scoggins asked. "A more direct route to Los Angeles would be on the Southern Pacific that runs a few miles north of here."

"A scheduling problem. There was too much traffic on the SP at the time, so I routed it to the El Paso and Southwestern."

"How could something that large simply vanish?" Scoggins asked, ignoring the food on his plate. "I mean, after all, it couldn't go any place where there weren't rails."

"Unless they were unloaded and carted off in trucks or wagons. But the train was never found, either. And don't think there wasn't a massive search between El Paso and southern California."

Scoggins shook his head as he resumed eating. "That

makes no sense. Sounds to me like somebody was paid off to keep his mouth shut. Somebody knows where they went."

"Of course somebody does, but company officials and railroad detectives have yet to find out who or where."

"If they weren't on the main line, doesn't the company know the locations of all the sidings and rail yards where they could have switched off?"

"Of course. All the major rail lines were contacted to be on the look-out for the two boxcars and the locomotive. Do you have any idea how many boxcars there are in this country? Thousands. And they're constantly on the move. Whoever got those were apparently well-organized. They could have painted them over within the first twenty-four hours or stenciled false numbers on them. Maybe they were later burned on some siding and the wheel trucks buried. They could have been painted and run into some crowded rail yard at night where they're sitting empty right now, yet to be identified. The locomotive could have been dismantled for parts or scrap in some roundhouse. . . ."

"And the crew never turned up, either?"

Whitlaw shook his head. "Five men gone . . . engineer, fireman, brakeman, and two armed guards riding in the caboose."

"Good Lord!"

"I was part of the débris after the blast."

"What do you mean?"

"All the big shots were so frustrated, they finally looked around for someone to blame. Even though there was not a particle of evidence that I had anything to do with it, except to dispatch the train to the SP, then to the EP and SW, and on to its destination, a lot of pressure was put on me to resign. I resisted, and my supervisor and his assistant made my life a living hell, until I finally gave it up and retired. I'd earned a reasonable retirement I could live on if I was careful, but it rankled that I left under a cloud after all those years. Rumors got out and some were published in the papers that the theft had been an inside job and that I'd been fired, and all kinds of stuff. Even though I wasn't actually named, they as much as said that the dispatcher was in on the plot."

Scoggins had finished his meal and sat back in his chair, picking his teeth, a fascinated look on his weathered face.

"The shipment was insured, of course, and the buyers eventually got their money, but that brought the insurance company investigators into it."

"You think you can find those guns when nobody else has been able to?" Scoggins asked.

"It's doubtful." Whitlaw shrugged. "But at least I'm in the right place where I can look, and I'm a long way from anybody who knew me or thinks I was in on it. I got tired of people looking at me like I was a thief."

The waiter arrived to refill Scoggins's coffee mug, and Whitlaw ordered a wedge of apple pie for dessert.

"I guess there's some good in everything," Whitlaw mused. "About the time I was forced out, my wife, Jane, was diagnosed with a malignant tumor. So I then had time to stay home and take care of her, once the doctors realized the cancer was terminal."

"You've held up under all that remarkably well," Scoggins said with undisguised admiration.

"Thanks. That's just the short version of the story," Whitlaw replied. There was no point in going into any of the more personal details of his life. He thought of the widow from a farm who had come by his house in town a week after Jane's funeral to "console" him. He had been so starved for love and intimacy, he had fallen into a brief affair with her, all the time realizing she was not someone he would ever marry. He dared not lead her into thinking their relationship would result in matrimony, but he lacked the courage to be blunt and hurt her feelings. Instead, pleading vague health concerns, he'd told her the doctor had ordered him to a warm, dry climate. He'd put his house in the hands of a broker, packed a bag, and caught a train to El Paso and then on to Columbus.

He was still vigorous at sixty-four, but found he could control his sexual urges if he saw no attractive women. Good-looking, available women in Columbus, New Mexico, were as rare as the blizzards he'd left behind. A dark young Mexican girl danced in a local saloon, but she had a live-in boy friend. It was rumored that two prostitutes lived in town and worked the soldiers at Camp Furlong, but he had never set eyes on either of them. It was almost with a sense of relief that he discovered he was beginning to lose his potency. Of all the ensnaring weaknesses of man, this was one that had plagued him the most. Maybe he was finally conquering it. He smoked a pipe occasionally. Except for a few drunken sprees in his youth, he'd always been a moderate drinker. Gambling had simply never held any allure for him. Perhaps if he'd thrown over his job and gone to the Klondike in '98. . . . But a man already had to have gold fever in order to do that.

As the two men walked back outside and headed down the rutted street, Whitlaw smiled to himself. *Damned if I don't sound like the Pharisee in the temple, thanking God in a loud voice that I'm not like other men who have all these disgusting vices. But it's a good thing every man doesn't have every weakness, or who would stand a chance before the Almighty?*

"Tell you what," Scoggins broke into his thoughts, "I've got to go check on my men to make sure they've got those

Ben-A's cleaned and oiled. Got a test-firing scheduled for tomorrow, and I'll have their hides if those machine-guns aren't in perfect working order."

"I'd like to watch that."

"Come along. It's scheduled for Oh Nine Hundred about a quarter mile south of camp."

"I've read where some military experts are calling machine-guns 'the ultimate weapon'," Whitlaw said.

"The same thing was said about the Gatling gun a few years back, and the repeating rifle before that, even as far back as the crossbow. But these Ben-A's are pretty fearsome weapons. They can fire seven hundred rounds a minute when they're working right."

"What did you call them?"

"We call 'em Ben-A's, short for *Benet-Mercie,* a French-designed gun the U.S. Army adopted in Nineteen Ten. It has only twenty-five parts to the whole assembly and it weighs only twenty-seven pounds. That's the good part. They're tricky to load, and they're so tightly put together that the men have to work over the extractor and the sear with emery paper to give them enough tolerance to work on full automatic. They're light to carry in the field, but the recoil is wicked and makes them hard to hold on target." The two men paused near a small adobe building. "Oh . . . you might want to bring some ear plugs, too."

"I'll make some or put my fingers in my ears." Whitlaw gestured at the heavy padlock on the plank door of the thick adobe building. "You think somebody is going to steal these things?"

"Just to remove temptation. One of these machine-guns sells across the border for at least six hundred dollars."

"I see."

"By the way, your story about those missing rifles fascinates me. As long as you're learning to fly, what say we follow the rails and go looking for any trace of your missing train? We can fly low and cover a lot of miles in a hurry. Might spot something from the air that was missed from the ground."

"Great idea."

"I'll see you in the morning, then."

"*Adiós.*" Whitlaw strode away toward the second hotel where he lived in a rented room. He might have looked back at Scoggins one more time if he had known this was the last time he'd see his friend alive.

Chapter Three

The distant *clang* of a brass bell followed by an explosive burst of pent-up steam penetrated Jim Whitlaw's consciousness. He stirred in his sleep and came partially awake. The "drunkard's special", as the midnight train from El Paso was locally known, usually didn't wake him. But lately he'd been sleeping with the window of his second-story hotel room open a foot to admit some fresh air.

He lay listening for a few seconds, wondering who, if anyone, was getting off or on. Not likely any of the soldiers from Camp Furlong would be among the passengers, since they usually weren't granted passes to town during the week. But Columbus was a regular stop on the El Paso & Southwestern for mail and freight as well as passengers.

Stretching his lean body, he rolled over and allowed his mind to go into neutral as the *whoof! whoof!* of the accelerating locomotive began receding into the distance.

It seemed he'd been asleep only a short time when blasts of gunfire woke him. He was instantly alert. More shots. They came from the direction of the railroad, as near as he could tell. Something definitely wrong. He was out of bed and pulling on his pants when he wondered briefly if there had been some deadly argument at the town's only saloon. But he dismissed this idea as he fumbled under the bed for his shoes. Too much gunfire for a saloon brawl. He glanced at the window, but only blackness showed outside. No moonlight. There was no electricity in Columbus and military requests for gas street lights had been routinely turned down.

Shirt in hand, he sprang to the window, standing to one side, just in case. He could see muzzle flashes in the street a block away to the south. There were hoof beats and the sounds of men shouting. He wished he were armed. But he hadn't even owned a gun since he'd carried a Smith & Wesson pocket pistol during his years as a conductor. Judging from the volume of the large caliber gunfire he was hearing, the little .32 caliber would have been of little use anyway. As it was, he felt completely helpless.

He fumbled his way out the door into the hallway. The flickering light of a candle showed the face of a wide-eyed woman with her head out of her door. "What is it? What's going on?" she wavered. "Why are they shooting off fireworks at this time of night?"

Farther along, a door slammed and a man in a nightshirt came out, carrying a lighted coal-oil lamp. He was puffy-eyed from heavy sleep. "Damnation! That's gunfire," he said. "I was in the war in Cuba. I know the sound of rifles when I hear 'em."

"Put that light out!" another voice cried.

"Don't matter. We're in the hallway," the man replied.

"Probably those Camp Furlong soldiers holding maneuvers," another voice said from the darkness.

Whitlaw brushed past them and bounded down the stairs, almost colliding with the Mexican bellboy who came out of his room under the stairway. "Eets Pancho Villa!" the boy cried. "I know eet!"

Whitlaw's stomach constricted. The boy could well be right. In spite of all the warnings and military preparations, that possibility hadn't even occurred to him. But now it sounded like a war had broken out. He eased open the front door to the porch and put one eye around the casing. Except for the tongues of fire lashing out from rifles and pistols, he could see nothing. He wondered how anyone could tell friend from foe. Suddenly he heard the staccato chatter of a machine-gun. After a short burst, it stopped abruptly, as if the gun had jammed. Sporadic rifle and handgun fire continued.

What should he do? His first instinct was to rush to the scene of the action to see what was happening. But immediately good sense took over. It would be foolhardy to run into the street and take a chance on being cut down by a stray bullet. He was one, aging, unarmed man. If this was an attack on the town and on Camp Furlong, there was nothing he could do about it. He'd be wiser to keep out of range and wait for the military to do their job. The intensity of the fighting couldn't last too long.

There were approximately ten guests in the Commercial Hotel and only five of them had awakened and come down to the lobby. The rest must be sound sleepers, as the racket of the firing was getting louder. He moved to the front window and took another look. The battle was working its way up the street toward the hotel. If these were, indeed, Villa's raiders, what was their objective? Sheer destruction? Maybe it was the bank, a couple of doors farther up the street. Whatever it was, Whitlaw wasn't about to get caught in this hotel lobby.

"They're coming toward the hotel!" he yelled at the few startled guests who were milling about uncertainly in their nightclothes. "Better get out the back way."

The salesman was the only one who responded as he made for the back room, carrying the lighted lamp. An older man and three women just stood staring in a state of shock. "I can't go out like this!" the lady with the candle quavered, indicating her long nightgown and bare feet.

Whitlaw felt a rush of anger at this stupidity. Then he recognized the same stunned irrationality he'd seen in others when a tornado came roaring out of a black Midwestern sky.

At that instant a bullet shattered the glass in the front door, breaking the paralysis. The women screamed and scattered toward the vacant registration desk. Whitlaw snatched a brass-headed walking stick from the hall tree just as Mexicans with rifles and bandoleers burst into the room from both the front and back. With his retreat cut off, he sprang for the stairs, instinctively going for the high ground. One of the raiders raised his carbine and fired. The bullet slammed into the wooden panel behind the crouching Whitlaw who was taking the stairs two at a time. The raiders were shouting in Spanish as the guests and hotel personnel scattered like chickens before a pack of wild dogs.

Whitlaw took advantage of the darkness in the upstairs hallway to duck into the first room he came to. Panting, he fumbled for a dead bolt inside the door, but there was none. Stumbling in the dark, he banged against the washstand, then encountered a straight chair that he dragged to the door and propped under the knob. It might hold them out long enough for him to make his escape out the window. They'd be upstairs in a few seconds, ransacking the rooms. The bloodlust was in their eyes, and even the prospect of sudden death under the withering fire of Army machine-guns wouldn't slow them down. Villa's men or not, they were as barbarous a crew of killers as he'd ever seen or heard. A scream sounded from the lobby, followed by three shots. Very likely executing the helpless women and maybe the hotel staff.

His nerves were wound tightly. A flicker of light caught his eye. Startled, he jumped back, raising the walking stick. The dim flash came from the window and threw a little light into the room. He stumbled across the room and yanked back the curtain. Directly across the street a hardware store was ablaze. With a whoop, a Mexican in a large sombrero flung a half full can of kerosene onto the porch. The glass window shattered and the added fuel roared upward in flame, engulfing the front of the building.

Whitlaw watched for several seconds in fascination as the blaze lighted up the entire street. He could see to his right that the soldiers were fighting a running battle with the raiders. At least fifty men on both sides were within sight. No telling how many more were in the darkness or on other streets. The soldiers were all on foot, as were most of the raiders, even though a dozen or more were galloping up and down the street, firing pistols at everything that moved. The raiders were slowly advancing, or being pushed up toward the hotel. He put down the walking stick and raised the sash. The heat and smell of the burning hardware store were blown into his face. And the noise! Hell had broken loose below in the little town. A machine-gun again began to chatter, raking the packed dirt of the street as the gunner fired too low. But the bullets skipped up and he saw three Mexicans throw up their arms and crumple to the ground. The survivors ran for cover in the buildings on either side of the street.

The front porch roof was only about six feet below him, and he slid a leg over the sill. A shot from below shattered the pane just above his head and he was showered with fragments of glass as he tumbled back inside. He crawled back to the window ledge and peered out. The Mexican gunmen would have an easy target if he tried that again. He had to find another way out. Flaming débris, borne high on the night wind, was raining down on the hotel and already the porch roof was ablaze. He'd get to a room on the side of the building where there might be a fire escape in the shadows. Just then the doorknob rattled, and his heart jumped into his throat. He took two steps when a rifle butt splintered a panel of the door. Whitlaw leapt across the bed and flattened himself against the wall. An arm appeared through the shattered panel and knocked away the braced chair. The next second the door flew open and a Mexican bandit came in. He caught the brass head of the walking stick full in the nose with all of Whitlaw's weight behind it. The man's head snapped back and he dropped the carbine. Whitlaw followed up with a kick to the groin and felt a fine spray of blood from the bandit's nose as he doubled over. One more hard kick sent the Mexican reeling backward out the door where he tumbled over the railing and down into the lobby.

Whitlaw grabbed the carbine and pulled back into the shadowed hallway as he heard the sounds of scuffling a few yards away. "That's all I've got!" a man yelled flinging out a handful of silver coins that rang on the bare floor. A Mexican soldier ignored the slamming door and scrambled on his hands and knees to retrieve the money.

Now was his chance. Whitlaw dashed for the door of a room farther down the hallway. He reached the room that was on the side of the building and wrenched the knob. It was locked.

"B'God, you'll not find a farthing in m'pockets!" a voice yelled.

Whitlaw turned to face the voice and sounds of a scuffle, working the bolt of the rifle. An empty cartridge casing tinkled onto the floor as he slammed the bolt home, praying there was a new live round in the chamber.

Two bandits were dragging a short, stocky man from his room, one on each arm. Whitlaw had never shot a man before in his entire sixty-four years, and he suddenly had qualms of conscience about pulling the trigger on these bandits.

The stocky man gave a sudden lunge, broke free, and ran toward the stairs. One of the Mexicans raised his pistol to shoot him in the back. Whitlaw fired the carbine from the hip. The roar was deafening in the confined space. The bandit doubled over and crumpled. Whitlaw hit the floor and rolled to one side—right under the legs of the fleeing man, who crashed down heavily on top of him. Whitlaw struggled to free himself while he worked the bolt of the rifle. The other bandit's gun went off. The man on top yelled and finally got himself untangled. Whitlaw slammed the bolt forward and down, threw the barrel up at an angle, and yanked the trigger. Yellow flame spurted in the semidarkness. Hit high in the chest, the bandit staggered back against the wall and slowly dropped as he convulsively squeezed off a last shot that blasted into the floor.

Whitlaw sprang to his feet and grabbed the stranger by the shirt. "I don't know who you are, mister, but it's time we got out of here!" he yelled in his ear. At least the man was not still in his pajamas.

The sound of breaking glass was followed by a *whoosh!*, and a sheet of flame ballooned out the open door of a room down the hall. The dry, wooden hotel was going up like a cardboard box in a high wind.

"This way!" he yelled, dragging the man to the last room on the hall where the door stood ajar. Inside, the window was open and the curtains ablaze. Snatching at the un-burned portion, Whitlaw yanked and flung them aside. The iron ladder of a fire escape ran alongside at an angle just below the window. "Out!" He pushed the stocky man ahead of him.

"I'll not stand on the order uv our goin'," the man said in his lilting dialect. He was out the window and three steps down before Whitlaw got one long leg over the sill.

They were on the side of the building, but had enough light from the blazing structures to see very well. They dropped to the ground, one at a time, and Whitlaw handed him the walking stick he had retrieved from the floor as they fled.

The stranger hefted the stick. "Good balance for a shillelagh," he remarked, smacking it into the palm of his other hand.

"What?"

"Nothing. Where are we going?"

"Just stay between these buildings to the street. Get moving!" He pushed the shorter man ahead of him. "There's an adobe wall in the next block. We can hide behind it until this dies down."

"What am I looking for? What's adobe?"

"I'll lead." Whitlaw elbowed his way ahead. The noise of the battle still raged behind them. Shadowy figures could be seen flitting between the buildings.

When they vaulted over the four-foot wall, they saw instantly that some scattered fighting was going on only fifty yards away.

"We can't stay here. Move."

A hundred yards farther, the two men ducked into a wooden privy behind a residence. Whitlaw looked out the crescent cut in the door.

"Whew! Smells worse than a pig farm in here," the man gasped.

"Keep your voice down. You're lucky to be able to smell

anything. You came mighty close to being killed back there."

Whitlaw pulled a match from his pocket and struck it against the rough wood wall. A strong odor of sulphur displaced the other smell for a few seconds as Whitlaw held the flame low to examine the rifle.

"Damn! Empty. I should have checked that Mex's bandoleer. Too late now." He dropped the dying match and it went out. "Well, I can still use it as a club," he added, shoving home the open bolt.

They stood side-by-side in the darkness for another several minutes while Whitlaw watched and listened, his breathing and heart rate gradually slowing. The staccato blasting of more than one machine-gun came to their ears, somewhat muffled by the wooden walls of the outhouse. Another half hour slowly dragged by. Neither man spoke for fear of being detected by the raiders who were still running through the streets and yards.

Finally the sounds of combat began to lessen. Whitlaw unlatched the door and pushed it open a crack, gratefully sucking in the fresh outside air. Except for a few sporadic shots and the sounds of galloping horses, the battle seemed to have ended. The firelight was brighter than ever with flames from the Commercial Hotel leaping high over the roofs of nearby buildings. How many more structures were burning, he couldn't tell.

"Let's go," he said to the man behind him. The only gunfire they could hear now was rapidly receding into the west, as if men on horseback were carrying the fight away. The machine-guns had fallen silent.

Whitlaw led the way south toward the railroad tracks, but kept in the shadows of buildings, away from the firelight. Here and there were lumps of clothing in the streets that contained corpses. He had the strangest sensation between his shoulder blades that one of these men was going to rise up and fire one last bullet at him as he went by.

By the time they reached the railroad crossing, Whitlaw felt they were safe. There was enough light from the fires to see that the area was manned by only a few American civilians and soldiers from Camp Furlong. Two soldiers carried one of the lightweight machine-guns, being careful not to touch the hot barrel. Another man trailed, limping, and swinging a half empty metal ammunition box by one handle.

Whitlaw was able to see much better, then realized the eastern sky was beginning to lighten. Another day was coming up over the horizon as if nothing had happened. Whitlaw, now that the danger was apparently over and the attackers had been driven off, felt himself sagging with a reaction that was more than fatigue.

Some distance away could be heard the voice of a noncom calling for his men to form up so he could take roll call. Whitlaw came up alongside the two soldiers who were carrying the machine-gun. "Where's Lieutenant Scoggins?"

The private turned an uncomprehending look his way and shook his head.

"Wilford Scoggins, officer of the machine-gun company . . . have you seen him?" Whitlaw asked, trying to penetrate the man's dazed mind.

"Yeah, I heard ya the first time," the soldier replied. "The bastards gunned him down." He jerked his head over his shoulder. "He's back there with the medic, but I don't see how nobody but God can help him now."

Whitlaw handed the stranger his empty carbine and set off up the street with long strides. Dawn light and firelight brightened the scene as Whitlaw found his friend stretched on his back, surrounded by three soldiers. Whitlaw went to one knee by the medic who had ripped open the soggy green uniform shirt and was holding a compress to a chest wound. But it was the color of Scoggins's face that told him all he needed to know. The medic turned a sweat-streaked face to Whitlaw and shook his head. The lieutenant's breathing was hoarse and ragged. The glazed eyes recognized no one. It was too late for good byes.

Whitlaw watched silently for several seconds, then got to his feet, heartsick, and walked away several slow paces, to stand looking at the reddening eastern sky. He was oblivious to the sounds of voices, crackling flames, crashing timbers collapsing into ruined buildings, the sight of dead bodies littering the streets, the light dawn breeze that carried the odors of burning wood, fresh horse manure, and spent gunpowder. Many things he thought of then. He had run to Columbus to escape his own past, and to find some tranquility in his retirement. For a few months he'd been successful. As a man grew older, he should have some surcease of sorrow and pain in his declining years—a period of peace, knowing he had done his best for himself, and his family, happy for the future of his children and grandchildren.

Lieutenant Scoggins had certainly taken the risk of choosing a dangerous profession, but thirty-nine was still too young to die. True, he'd joked fatalistically about dying young in an airplane crash. But this was a needless death at the hands of a bunch of Mexican rebels. A man's death should mean something, or should at least be heroic or dignified. Lieutenant Scoggins would certainly be considered a hero for giving his life defending the town of Columbus. But this would be only a footnote in history—just another aborted border raid by a bunch of crazed rebels, forgotten in a few short years by all except his immediate relatives, or the survivors of this fight. Luckily he had no wife or children, but he did have parents in Nebraska, and he had mentioned a brother and sister. How senseless all this seemed. He felt tears welling up in his eyes. Were they tears for Scoggins, or for himself and his own bleak future?

"I've not made your official acquaintance, sir." The voice with the strange dialect was at his elbow. "I'll be thankin' ye for savin' m'life."

Whitlaw looked around distractedly. He'd forgotten all about the presence of this stubby little man. "Yes, yes. You're quite welcome." Then added: "Jim Whitlaw." He thrust out a hand.

The short man gripped it. "I'm Tommy Glasheen, from County Kerry, Ireland." He stared intently at Whitlaw. "And it's yourself I've been sent to meet."

Chapter Four

Whitlaw was as irritated as if he'd been awakened from a dream by the ringing of a salesman. "Whatever you want, it can wait," he said curtly. He couldn't imagine anything so important that it would supersede what had just taken place. For the first time he actually looked closely at the short man who said his name was Tommy Glasheen. The man's sleeve was soaked in blood, which had already crusted and dried on the back of his left hand.

"You're hurt," Whitlaw managed to say in a somewhat gentler tone. "Why didn't you say something earlier?"

"Savin' m'breath altogether was top o' my list at the time," Glasheen replied, glancing ruefully at his sleeve. He started to raise the arm, but winced and let it drop back to his side.

"Let's get a medic to look at that. When did it happen? Did you catch a bullet?"

Glasheen nodded. "I was in the process o' fallin'," he said. "If you hadn't rolled under my legs in that hallway, I'd 'a' caught the bullet in the back of m'neck or head," he said. " 'Twas only the big muscle in my upper arm that it clipped."

"Did the slug go through?"

"I don't know, but a taste o' poteen would likely cool off the devil's own pitchfork that's burning it."

As they talked, Whitlaw took him by the good arm and

directed him back to the medic who was just then rinsing his bloody hands with a canteen of water. Two soldiers were lifting the body of Lieutenant Scoggins onto a stretcher. Whitlaw looked briefly at the remains and said a silent good bye.

"Can you take a look at this man's wound?"

The medic dried his hands on a dirty towel, then took the cuff of the bloody shirt and, with a yank, tore it upward all the way to the shoulder.

"*Auugh!* There goes m'best shirt!" Glasheen moaned. "And now it's me only shirt," he added, glancing at the still-burning pile of timbers a block away that had been the Commercial Hotel.

"Just grooved the surface," the medic said. "Maybe got a tiny bit of the muscle fiber. Hold still," he added, yanking the cork from a bottle of alcohol in his kit and splashing some into the wound to cleanse and disinfect it.

The bobbing of his Adam's apple was the only sign Glasheen even felt the sting.

"Hmm . . . pretty nasty looking. Let me take a few stitches to hold it together."

While Whitlaw looked away, the medic took advantage of the increasing light of dawn to close the gash with a curved needle and surgical thread.

"There. If that should start to fester, come see me. It'll be sore as a boil for a while, and, if it got a little nerve, you could have some numbness later in that spot." He turned to go. "If you can find a clean cloth, wrap a bandage around that."

Glasheen slipped gingerly out of the shirt and tore the bloody sleeve completely off. His broad chest was matted with curly black hair. "Throbs like a toothache," he remarked, pulling the shirt back on.

"Might help if you carried it up in a sling. Here, let me try this." Whitlaw shucked out of his vest and ripped it apart at the seams, fashioning a crude sling that he tied around Glasheen's thick neck.

"How does that feel?"

"You're an angel in disguise," Glasheen sighed in gratitude.

"We'll get something better later."

"I got in on the midnight train from El Paso," Glasheen said. "B'God, what a welcome! Or do the white lights roar like that every night?" he asked, a gleam in his bloodshot eyes.

In spite of his somber mood, Whitlaw couldn't help but smile. He suspected Glasheen was probably something of a blatherskite, but a charming one, nonetheless. "You're looking a mite peaked," he said. "Need to get some food and drink into you." He spoke to his own need as much as to the Irishman's.

"I don't suppose there's a place in Columbus that serves Guinness?"

Whitlaw shook his head.

"I thought not."

Whitlaw laughed aloud at the plaintive look. "This place may seem like it, but it's not the end of the world. Come on. I know Colonel Slocum. We'll get something to eat at the mess shacks on post. In fact, it looks like the Army is feeding several of the townspeople down there now."

The cooks had set up something akin to an emergency feeding station for military and civilian alike.

Glasheen and Whitlaw sat down with the wives and children of some of the officers at the long wooden table to spoon up some hot soup. Whitlaw put down the empty rifle he'd gotten back from Glasheen, while the Irishman laid the walking stick on the table.

Litter bearers and Model T Ford pickup trucks were bringing in the dead and wounded. A hospital tent was being erected to serve as a first aid station.

Whitlaw saw nothing of the several hotel guests who'd been in the lobby with him. Their murdered remains had very likely burned up in the fire. As hungry as he was, he wasn't able to eat more than one bowl of the thin soup and a half piece of bread before his revulsion at the carnage, the heat, and the flies began to make him queasy. In his sixty-four years he'd witnessed several violent deaths, mostly from accidents on the railroad. However, he'd never been in a battle where men purposely shot or stabbed each other. The ugly brutality of it showed him a side of humanity he wished he'd never seen. His own killing of the two raiders, done in the heat of the fight, didn't yet bother him when he thought of it. Perhaps it never would. Self-preservation was a strong instinct.

It was evident from the way the stocky Irishman was putting away the food that he suffered from no such qualms.

Whitlaw swung his legs over the bench and got up. "Meet me outside when you're done." He glanced at the angle of the sun, then reached for his watch. Luckily the gold Elgin he'd carried all those years on the railroad had been in his pants pocket when he jumped into his clothes, or it would have been destroyed along with everything else in his hotel room. His savings were safe in the bank the raiders had not reached.

"You got any other clothes?" he asked when Glasheen came up beside him.

"None but these," he replied. "If the hotel safe is intact, then m'money is there. And a letter of credit."

They strode away from Camp Furlong, across the railroad tracks and back up Main Street toward the smoldering ruins of their hotel and the hardware store. Two young Army officers came walking toward them. "Major Tompkins and Captain Smyser took off after them with more than fifty men from H and F Troops," one of the officers said to the other, pointing west. "Got 'em on the run. Hope they don't stop at the border."

"If our men are in hot pursuit, we don't have to," the other replied as they passed out of earshot.

"It appears the only saloon in Columbus is open for business a little earlier than usual," Whitlaw said. "Care to join me for a drink? I'm curious as to why you were sent to find me."

Glasheen licked his lips. "Nothing like a hot fire, a loss of blood, and some salty soup to put an edge on a man's thirst," he said. "I'd be obliged to have a pint with ye."

"Luckily I always keep my billfold in my pants pocket, so I'm buying." Whatever this foreigner had to say would at least keep his mind off last night's horror. Whitlaw was still feeling a little dazed. Except for his sore muscles and the turmoil he saw all around him, he might have been able to dismiss the whole thing as some realistic nightmare.

A few minutes later they were seated at a corner table by a window. Glasheen took a long pull at his mug, then wiped the foam from his lip. "I needed that," he sighed. "Now to business. . . ." He proceeded to relate the background and purpose of his mission.

Whitlaw went from curious to amazed. "How in the world did anyone in Ireland find out about me?"

Glasheen shook his head. "I didn't ask. They're an international bunch, and have contacts everywhere. Some of the leaders spend most of their time in New York, or soliciting and lecturing to raise funds all over this country."

"Probably got the information about me from that series of articles syndicated on the wire services two years ago. But how did they know I had come to New Mexico?"

"I'm guessin' Donahue had someone go to the last place you lived and inquire, or maybe to the office of the Union Pacific. Rory said I'd have no trouble finding you in this tiny village." He nodded toward the window. " 'Tis hardly bigger than the village where I'm from in Kerry, except that it's dry and flat and dusty here. The boys who're planning this uprisin' have quite a network," he added a little proudly. "And they've got the will. The only things holding us back from breaking free of the British lion are . . . we're not all of the same mind on just how to proceed, and the lack of sufficient arms and ammunition for all the volunteer fighters." He paused to take another swallow of his beer. "You can't do anything about Irish pride and disagreement. But you can help by selling us that stash of rifles and cartridges."

"I'm sorry to break the news, but you've made a long trip for nothing," Whitlaw replied. "If your bosses think I had something to do with stealing those weapons, they're absolutely wrong. I was falsely accused in the newspapers. I have no more idea where that trainload of guns went than you do. In fact, when I was pressured to take my pension from the UP, I moved here thinking I might get a lead on where those guns went, since they vanished somewhere between here and the Arizona border."

A look of consternation came over Glasheen's face. "I . . . b'God . . . well, now. . . ." He sat back in his chair, rubbing his left arm with his right hand.

"Besides, I don't know what would make your bosses think those guns would be mine to sell, even if I knew where they were. Technically, I guess, they would belong to the insurance company that paid for their loss." Whitlaw downed the remainder of his beer and signaled the bartender for another. "Or maybe grand theft is but a venial sin to the leaders of your uprising." Until just this minute, he'd never really considered what he might do with the guns if he found them. He assumed they would be turned over to the proper owners—the railroad, the insurance company, the buyers—someone. What mattered to him was the public clearing of his name. Of course, if he found them hidden somewhere intact, how would he convince anyone that he hadn't conspired to have them stolen, and then had a change of heart later? And what about the train crew? If their skeletons were also discovered, he might be accused of being in on a murder plot.

He frowned as the bartender set a full glass in front of him and took away the empty. He might be better off if the guns and the train never turned up, and the whole episode eventually toppled over into history as one of the great unsolved mysteries of Western folklore. He'd been over the possibilities a thousand times in his mind. Although he had no reason, other than a hunch, for thinking so, he was of the opinion that the guns had long since passed into the hands of Mexican rebels.

"B'God, you're beginning to look like a man with weighty matters on his mind," Glasheen said, sipping a fresh beer. The shock, the loss of blood, and the lack of sleep had made him pale and clammy for a time. But, after the food and drink, his face was beginning to regain a more ruddy hue.

"I was only imagining what I might do with those guns if I had 'em. It never occurred to me to think of them as my own."

"They'd probably come under the laws of salvage, like a

derelict on the high seas," Glasheen ventured. He glanced around to be sure no one was listening, then lowered his voice slightly. "But you can be honest. I've never been known to betray a trust. You have those rifles hidden in some safe place, now, don't you? Your secret is safe with me. I'm prepared to offer you a lot of cash, take them off your hands, and out of the country."

Whitlaw chuckled and shook his head at this persistent little Irishman. "I've never had a good poker face. When I say I don't know where they are, I really don't. I'm not lying or trying to conceal something. Look, it's been two years since they were stolen. It's not news any more. The buyer has collected his insurance on the lost shipment, and all but a few people have probably forgotten about it. Don't you think I would have gotten rid of them by now? In the four or five years this Mexican revolution has been going on, there has been a constant flow of illegal gun sales across the border, mostly by way of El Paso. If I was one of those American profiteers, don't you think I would have disposed of those stolen weapons for a lot of money? I wouldn't still be sitting here in this dusty hole waiting for an Irishman to offer me a deal . . . an Irishman I didn't even know was coming."

Glasheen was somewhat abashed by this reasoning and did not reply. "Well," he finally said, "ye've got an honest mug, I'll give y'that. If you're weavin' a tale, I can't tell it."

"On my wife's grave, that's the truth," Whitlaw said, swearing on the most sacred thing he could think of.

"All right, then, but what am I to tell Rory Donahue and the others when I return empty-handed? It won't go well with me. At the very least, they'll think I'm a gullible fool."

"They're the ones who are foolish for believing hearsay."

"Blessed if I don't think there's some reason for

m'comin' to America besides just gettin' m'hide punctured, then going right back home. I just wish I knew what that reason was."

Whitlaw was beginning to feel more relaxed and leaned back in his chair, stretching out his legs and yawning. "Just maybe the Lord thought that you'd worked hard all your life and deserved a little reward while you're still on this earth."

"My wife and family have been my reward."

"True enough, but they're not with you now. Haven't you enjoyed the trip so far, and seen some of this big beautiful country? When I rode the trains for years, I never tired of seeing that rolling countryside during all the changes of season. Don't tell me you traveled all this way blindfolded."

"Right you are. After I got over worryin' about the U-boats sinkin' m'ship, and then a bout o' seasickness, I did enjoy m'self. I was wishin' Ann was with me. And I was absolutely amazed at how big this country is. What a lot of unused land!"

"See there? Now I'm thinking you don't have to rush right home and report the bad news. You can just send a wire, then stick around and take your time traveling back. Maybe see some more of the States."

"They're not paying me to have a free vacation," Glasheen demurred.

"Then tell Donaho, or whatever his name is, that the revolt will have to go on without you, because you've been shot and need time to recover."

"You're not makin' light o' the Irish struggle for independence, are ye?" Glasheen asked a little testily.

"Not at all. I'm totally in sympathy with it. But you're a long way from that. Right here and now we've got a revolution on our doorstep, and I expect all hell to break loose when Washington gets the news about this." He drank the rest of his beer, noting the Irishman's empty glass.

"I'd best get up and out of here. As tired as I am, one more beer would put me to sleep."

Just as the two men emerged from the saloon into the sunlight, they ran into Justin Potter, a desk clerk from the Commercial Hotel. He was wearing a narrow brim, black hat. His gray vest and white shirt were grimed with soot. Potter's eyes, behind the dusty magnifying lenses of his glasses, were wide and stunned. "Mister Whitlaw . . . Mister Glasheen . . . ," he greeted them, nodding with the habitual formality he used behind the hotel registration desk. "Did you hear about Missus Parks?"

"No. Was she killed or captured?" Whitlaw asked. Mrs. Parks was the night telephone operator.

"She stayed at her post when the attack started and was cut with flying glass when bullets shattered the windows of her little cubbyhole of an office," the clerk said, spreading his hands in wonder. "She blew out the lamp and managed to crank up her counterpart in Deming, then gave a blow by blow description of the battle for nearly two hours. She's a real heroine."

"B'God, I'm believin' there were a lot of heroes around here last night," Glasheen said, looking at Whitlaw.

"What about yourself, Potter?" Whitlaw asked.

"I was on the night shift," he said, "and, after I checked in Mister Glasheen and another man who got off the late train, I went into the back room and lay down on my cot. I was sound asleep when all that started, but got out the back door and went to hide my wife and son in a field behind the house before the raiders got there. Missus Bartlett was killed, you know," he added.

"I wonder what the hell they wanted, anyway?" Whitlaw said.

"Mainly the horses at Camp Furlong," Potter answered. He seemed to have spent the morning gathering information and stories from the various survivors and military officers. He had a reputation as the town gossip. "They turned a lot of the horses loose, but the quick work of the riflemen drove them away from the stables and toward the mess shacks. That's where the cooks got into the act." He paused as if waiting for Whitlaw and Glasheen to ask what happened. Considering the dullness of his daily clerical routine, it was no wonder to Whitlaw that he was getting a great deal of satisfaction out of being the first to spread the details of this exciting night.

"What'd the cooks do?"

"They were already up by four thirty, brewing coffee and fixing breakfast. They keep shotguns handy to bag rabbits and such to supplement the fare. Well, sir, they opened up on those *Villistas* with the scatter-guns, and the ones who didn't go down, took to their heels. But they ran right toward Lieutenant Scoggins and his machine-gunners. They didn't have a chance."

"B'God, they opened up a hornets' nest when they expected a honeycomb," Glasheen said.

"But that's not all," Potter continued. "The machine-gunners didn't worry about hitting the cooks since they were behind those thick adobe walls. When the *Villistas* tried to break down the door to the mess shacks to get shelter, the cooks were ready. Slung scalding coffee on them as they came in, and then the cook's helper laid into 'em with that axe he uses to chop firewood."

"Damn!"

"Yeah," Potter continued with relish. "They were all over blood and guts and pieces of skull as big as your hand. I saw one of them. Had the hair still attached."

Whitlaw felt the blood drain from his face at the gruesome description. This had been a very brutal battle.

"Thank God, there were only seventeen people killed on our side," Potter continued. "Nine civilians and eight soldiers. Several others wounded, though, and some horses killed. But the *Villistas* took quite a hit."

"What about your hotel safe?" Whitlaw asked, trying to change the subject.

"Well, it'll be at least tomorrow before that fire cools off enough for us to get to it and see if anything inside was scorched. It's supposed to be fireproof, but we'll see."

Whitlaw thought Potter was probably still in shock, judging from the clerk's wide eyes and rapid-fire dialogue. This was not his usual demeanor.

"Well, I'm off to the train station," the clerk said with a wave. "Edwin Van Camp, the Associated Press telegrapher from El Paso, was in town last night because of a tip his boss got that something was about to happen. He's down there now, wiring off his story. I want to make sure he has all the details." The little man went striding away, his hat set squarely on his head. "Oh, by the way," he said, stopping several yards off. "If you need a place to stay the night, you might try the Columbus Hotel. I think they're full up, but Walter might be able to squeeze you in somewhere."

"Thanks. We'll find something."

When the little clerk was out of earshot, Whitlaw said: "I've got an idea we might be able to use Lieutenant Scoggins's little adobe house overnight. Let's go see."

They found First Lieutenant Clarence Benson, Scoggins's sometime roommate, stuffing clothing and personal items into his duffel when they pushed open the door and entered. He looked up.

"Sorry. Didn't know anybody was here," Whitlaw said.

69

"Just packing up some of Wil's personal things to send to his family," Benson said with a sad shake of his head.

"Are they going to have any sort of service here before they ship his body?"

"Everyone who was killed here will be buried here. If relatives want to come and disinter them later, they can. As to any funeral services, I don't know yet." He dropped a straight razor kit and shaving mug into the bag.

"Are you leaving, too?"

Lieutenant Benson nodded. "I've been on detached duty for nearly a month anyway, so I'm just going to go ahead and move onto the post. Colonel Slocum expects President Wilson to finally send a force across the border in retaliation now. I figure my troop to be one of the first to go."

"Who owns this house?"

"The vice president of the bank, Mister Clifford Rondell." He paused and looked at them. "Wil told me you were living at the Commercial Hotel. If you and your friend need somewhere to stay, you can have this place. Cheaper than the Columbus Hotel, and the rent's paid to the end of the month. If Rondell asks, tell him I'm subletting it to you." He gestured around at the bare, cracked walls of whitewashed adobe brick. "If you don't mind sharing the place with a rattler now and then, and aren't squeamish about shaking a scorpion out of your boots in the morning, then it should suit you fine. Beats sleeping out in the open, or in a tent."

"There are no serpents in Ireland," Glasheen remarked wistfully, glancing around the room as if he half expected to see a rattler poke his head up through a knothole in the board floor.

The lieutenant introduced himself to Glasheen. "How's the wound?" he asked.

"You Yanks are mighty kind. When a man sheds his blood in battle, the ladies fawn over him and the men offer him drinks like he's some kind of hero." Glasheen grinned.

"It's probably your Irish dialect that charmed the ladies," Benson guessed.

"And they know their virtue is safe around an old man like me," Glasheen said, tossing the walking stick onto a bed and rubbing the lower part of his wounded arm.

The three men chatted until Benson finished cleaning out his few belongings and left.

Whitlaw hefted the empty rifle. "Guess I should have given this to Benson. I don't have any use for it without ammunition."

"It's not one of their standard Springfields," Glasheen said, "so the soldiers probably don't have any ammunition for it, either."

For the first time, Whitlaw took a closer look at the weapon. His heart began to beat faster. "It's a Krag-Jorgensen, just like those that were declared surplus by the Army."

"And the same kind that were in the shipment that disappeared," Glasheen finished.

Whitlaw nodded. "Somewhere I had a list of the serial numbers on those rifles," he said. "I think it's in the hotel safe."

"Even if you knew that was one of the stolen weapons, how would that help?"

"All it would tell us is that at least some of the guns have found their way into the hands of the revolutionaries. And I'd already assumed that. But I know there are quite a number of these floating around on the market, so this could be one of those rifles that was sold across the border by profiteering American gun dealers."

Glasheen sat down on the low bed that was pushed against the opposite wall of the bedroom. "This time yesterday, I was eating supper and getting ready to board the train in El Paso," he said. "B'God, what a difference a day makes."

Whitlaw nodded, pulling off his shoes. "The sun's not even set yet, and I'm ready for bed. Must be getting old," he added, with a rueful grin.

Chapter Five

A sharp rap at the door startled Whitlaw, and he nearly spilled his coffee. Before he could move, Lieutenant Benson thrust his head inside. "Whitlaw, Colonel Slocum wants to see you in his office right away."

Still too keyed up to rest easily, Whitlaw had been up and dressed for an hour. "Do you know what he wants?"

"Nope. But I expect it has something to do with Wil Scoggins."

"Thanks, Lieutenant. Tell him I'll be right along."

Benson nodded and withdrew, latching the plank door behind him.

Glasheen stirred sleepily and sat up in bed in the next room. "Can't believe I slept this late," he said, glancing at the morning sun streaming through the window. "M'arm's stiffened up some, but it's not painin' me like I thought it would."

"Here's a cup of coffee. Pull on some clothes and we'll go see what Colonel Slocum wants."

"Have a seat, Whitlaw," Colonel Slocum said with no preliminaries. The commanding officer threw a curious glance at Tommy Glasheen who was standing to one side. "Who's this?"

"A friend of mine," Whitlaw answered. "From Ireland."

Slocum, looking preoccupied, didn't respond. Dark circles under his eyes testified to the strain of command and sleeplessness. The lines of his face seemed deeper and the mustache grayer than Whitlaw remembered.

"I'll get right to the point," Slocum said. "I sent for you because you were a good friend of Lieutenant Scoggins."

"Yes, sir."

"I'm sorry for your loss, but I'm even sorrier for my loss. He was a good officer and a good man. But, to tell you the truth, I half expected him to be killed in a smash-up of that damned flying contraption he insisted on playing around with." He paused in his pacing behind the desk to strike a match to a slim cigar he was holding. He blew a cloud of smoke at the ceiling and continued. "If Scoggins left a will, it must be with his parents back East or at a bank somewhere. We're sending all of his effects to his family, but I'm taking it upon myself to get rid of that airplane out there. I know for a fact that his family didn't approve of him flying, because he told me so himself. What I'm getting at is this . . . you can have that airplane if you want it. He was teaching you to fly it, wasn't he?"

"Yes, sir."

"Then I think he'd want you to have it. You can use it or sell it, or whatever."

Whitlaw was completely taken aback. "Well, of course, I'd love to have it, but. . . ." He paused. "Won't his family want the proceeds from the sale of it?"

Slocum waved his hand impatiently. "I'll deal with that. If they ask, they'll be informed it was damaged in the raid and I'm confiscating what's left to pay for rent on the hangar. I'm not so sure he didn't tell them he was renting the plane, anyway."

Whitlaw said nothing.

"Of course, it wasn't damaged, but you can have it on one condition . . . that you get the damned deathtrap out of my stable and off government property before any more of my officers get the notion they want to fly."

Whitlaw opened his mouth to reply, but was interrupted by the door bursting open and Lieutenant Benson entering. He saluted. "Sorry to bust in, Colonel, but there's a Maud Wright here. I think you need to see her right away." He seemed out of breath.

Whitlaw got up to leave.

"Stand by until I see what this is about," Slocum said, somewhat irritated.

Two enlisted men escorted a young woman into the office. Her full skirt was ripped off at mid-calf, and she was wearing a pair of sandals. It appeared her dark hair had been pulled back from her face and tied behind her head. She was sunburned and bore several fresh scratches on her bare arms and face.

"She was a captive of the *Villistas* for ten days before the raid," Lieutenant Benson said. "I want you to hear her story. Go ahead and tell the colonel what you told us."

She sagged into a chair the lieutenant held for her.

"My husband, Ray, and I own a ranch about a hundred twenty miles south of here," she began. "Been there since before all this revolution started . . . over six years now, and nobody's bothered us. We just mind our own business and get along. Well, a dozen horsemen rode up to the house the first of the month. Ray was gone . . . just me and the baby there. I been used to such visits and went out and invited them in for a drink and some food. I been there long enough that I can speak and understand a little Spanish, although I'm not good at it. But we'd been staying out of trouble with the different groups of irregulars by offering

75

such hospitality as we had. Well, this day, a Colonel Nicolas Hernández refused and said I was a prisoner of the Division of the North. . . ."

"Villa's bunch of revolutionaries in Chihuahua," Benson broke in.

Slocum frowned irritably at the interruption, keeping his eyes fixed on the woman seated before him.

"I was scared, but didn't do or say anything to provoke them. I just stood there with the baby in my arms, trying to talk calm. Pretty soon, Ray and a friend named Hayden come riding in and they were placed under arrest, too. Hernández's men drew their guns and made me give up my child to a Mexican woman who was with them. Then we were ordered to mount up and ride with them, while the Mexican woman stayed behind at the ranch house with my baby daughter. We rode hard all day and into the night until we got to the little settlement of Cave Valle. A bunch of other men were already camped there, and we all got a little sleep. In the morning, my husband and Hayden were taken to Villa. When they came back, Ray said Villa wouldn't tell them why we had been taken prisoner or what was going to happen to us."

She paused to reach gratefully for a cup of water Benson poured from his canteen for her.

Colonel Slocum leaned against the front of his desk with his arms folded and waited for her to continue.

"Shortly after, some men came and took Ray and Hayden away and I never saw them again. I heard later from some of this gang they'd been executed."

Whitlaw felt a twinge of sorrow for this woman, even as he admired her courage. She appeared to have been brought here without food or rest to tell her story to the commanding officer before another hour went by.

"The Mexicans cooked their breakfast over the camp-fires and ate without giving me anything, even though I was getting weak with hunger. Colonel Hernández told me Villa didn't want any food wasted on me because I was going to die a horrible death. He told me to mount up and said . . . 'We are going to ride all day and all night until we reach Columbus . . . if you live that long.' Well, you don't survive for years on a ranch in Mexico unless you learn to deal with hardship. I'm tougher than I look, and I was determined to keep up. If I'd collapsed or fallen back, they'd have shot me and left me for the buzzards. It took two days and nights of hard riding to reach the border. I lived on a few scraps of leftover food, and I never let on that I was near done in with exhaustion. Whenever we stopped briefly to rest the horses, I'd go from one officer to another and beg to be allowed to go back to my child. I was ignored. Finally I got to talk briefly with Villa himself. He put me off by telling me to go back and ask Hernández. A little later Colonel Hernández told me Villa admired my gameness and courage, and that he would probably set me free once their purpose in Columbus had been accomplished. I said . . . 'Colonel, what is your purpose?' He said . . . 'To burn and loot the town and kill every American there.' "

Slocum and Benson exchanged glances. "That confirms the information we found on one of the dead raiders," Slocum said.

"What information, sir?" Major Lindsley asked, coming into the office at that moment.

"A long letter from Villa to Emiliano Zapata telling him to bring his army north to join in an attack on the United States. According to the date on the letter, this had been planned as early as January 8th."

"Then a lot of those rumors were true," Lindsley said.

Slocum nodded. "The letter even set a six-month dead-line for concentrating their forces in northern Mexico, and said that Villa had sent out couriers to incite the populace against Americans."

"Bastard!" Benson breathed.

"Go on with your story, Missus Wright," Slocum urged.

"When we got to Columbus late at night, I was put under guard and then heard them giving commands just before hundreds of riders headed for the border. Villa himself headed up one of the columns."

"An eyewitness, if we needed any further proof!" Benson said.

Slocum held up his hand for silence and nodded for her to continue.

"Well, I heard a lot of firing and shouting, and you know the rest. When they came back across about dawn, I was taken along with them. We rode most of the day and finally stopped at a little mud hut village to attend the wounded. Villa came up and asked me if I wanted to return to the United States. 'If you would do me that favor,' I replied in polite Spanish. He told me to take my horse and leave. I didn't wait for a second invitation. I rode all evening and all night and finally got here just after dawn this morning. My horse and I were both nearly done in."

"You're a very lucky woman," Slocum said, looking at her with a softer expression than Whitlaw had ever seen on his face.

"I know," she nodded. "Ray is gone, but I'd sure like to go back to the ranch and see if my daughter is still there." She blinked back the tears that were filling her eyes.

"As soon as we feel it's safe, we'll get you there," Slocum replied. "First thing is to get you some hot food and a good rest. See to it, Benson."

"Yes, sir." He took Maud Wright's arm to help her from the chair.

"One more thing," Slocum said.

She stopped.

"What is Villa like?"

She seemed perplexed. "Well, he's a bowlegged, barrel-chested man who cuts a fine, dashing figure on horseback. But when he's afoot, he looks just like the short, brutal pigeon-toed Mex peasant that he is. I'd guess he's something under forty years old, dark hair and eyes, thick mustache, and wears a big sombrero. Oh, and he has all his men use red saddle blankets so he can distinguish them at a glance when they're riding with others."

"Is he intelligent?"

Maud paused, then said slowly: "If you mean is he cunning, the answer is yes. He can't read or write. He tries to bed any woman who takes his eye, even though I hear he's married. Like most Mexican men, he's full of machismo, however you want to interpret that. Unpredictable and brutal are two words that probably describe him best."

"Thank you, Missus Wright. I like to know my enemy," Slocum said, taking her hand. "You've helped us more than you can ever know, and the Army will not forget it."

Lieutenant Benson escorted Maud Wright out of the office and closed the door behind them.

"Remarkable woman," Colonel Slocum said quietly, staring at the closed door.

"That's a fact," Whitlaw agreed.

The remark seemed to break Slocum's reverie, and he again became aware of the presence of Whitlaw, Glasheen, and Major Lindsley. "Yes, what is it, Lindsley?" he asked in a tired voice.

His second in command approached with a handful of

yellow dispatches. "Telegrams, sir, from Washington, Fort Bliss, General Funston at Fort Sam Houston, and even two here from *The Chicago Tribune* and *The New York World* wanting more details of the raid . . . some human interest stuff."

"Let me see the official ones."

"Looks like things are really popping in D.C.," Lindsley said, handing over the dispatches. "President Wilson called a cabinet meeting to decide what to do about all this."

"Well, he can't ignore it, that's for sure. The whole country's yelling for Villa's head, just like you predicted."

Slocum took the telegrams and paced to the window where he read them by the better light. "They're not wasting any time. This says John J. Pershing is being named to lead a punitive expedition into Mexico." He looked up. "A good man, Pershing. I'll be glad to serve under him. Hard disciplinarian, but a real soldier. That's what it'll take on this campaign."

"Well, so much for Wilson's diplomacy," Whitlaw said.

Slocum nodded. "I wouldn't be in his shoes for all the tea in China," he said. "Wilson knows it's a lot easier to get into a shooting war than to get out of one. Carranza may be only the *de facto* president of Mexico, but you can bet he's going to look on this campaign as an invasion of his country and an act of war."

"Sir, in my opinion, Carranza should be glad we're helping his army rid the country of that damned bandit who's doing all he can to keep Carranza from becoming the official president of Mexico," Lindsley remarked.

"Carranza's proud. Thinks he can do it alone, and he probably could, given enough time," Slocum said, thoughtfully scanning the handful of messages. "Germany would like nothing better than to see the United States embroiled in a war with Mexico, so we won't jump into the European fight on the side of the Allies."

A few seconds of silence followed while Slocum finished reading. "Who's Captain Benjamin Delahauf Foulois?" Slocum queried, arching his brow. "Says here he's in charge of eight airplanes being sent by rail for reconnaissance duty."

"Only the most experienced man in the Army when it comes to piloting aircraft, sir," Lindsley replied. "Word is he was taught to fly by Orville Wright himself. Late thirties, tall, pipe-smoking, easy-going, very competent. You'd like him, sir. He was the first dirigible pilot. The only logical man to head up a squadron of fighting pilots and aircraft."

"*Humph!* Messenger boys and scouts," Colonel Slocum grunted. "We used to use Indians and half-breed civilians for such duty. And now I'm told one of those damned motorized kites costs the government more than six thousand dollars. No wonder Congress has passed a temporary tax on everybody's income."

"Gibraltar is about as temporary as a temporary tax," Whitlaw commented.

"Congress appropriated only about five hundred thousand dollars for the whole Army air squadron last year," Lindsley said, as if reciting statistics from the Congressional Record. Evidently realizing he sounded somewhat insubordinate, he hurried on: "Any replies to those wires, sir?"

"I'll draft up acknowledgments. These are mostly just information and instructions . . . they're not asking my advice. I'm to get my men ready to join the brigade when General Pershing gets here." He turned back from the window and suddenly realized Whitlaw and Glasheen were in the room. "You two still here? Nothing further I need you for. If you want that Jenny, get it out of the stable this afternoon

81

before any more cavalry arrive. We'll need all the stable space we can get until the troop moves out."

"Right, Colonel," Whitlaw replied, relieved to be dismissed from the presence of officialdom. He felt as if he were eavesdropping on this conversation, and he was not the least bit curious about the upcoming expedition. He'd find out more than he wanted to know during the next few days, anyway. His main problem, at the moment, was what to do with the airplane.

Outside in the sunshine, Whitlaw noticed Glasheen holding his wounded arm with his right hand. The flesh around the stitches appeared red and swollen. The Irishman was still wearing the shirt with only one sleeve, now grimed with soot and spotted with dried, brownish blood. He had neglected to put on the makeshift sling Whitlaw had fashioned from his vest.

"That wound looks infected. Let's let the medic take a look at it."

The same medic they'd seen the day before was on duty at the camp hospital. He snipped the stitches, reopened the gash, swabbed it liberally with a strong-smelling disinfectant, while Glasheen gritted his teeth silently. To Whitlaw, it looked like raw meat, oozing blood and coated with gray-green mold.

"I'm leaving this open to heal," the medic said. "You got a clean shirt you can wear over it to keep dirt off the dressing?"

Glasheen started to reply, but Whitlaw cut in: "I'll make sure he gets one."

The medic saturated several layers of gauze with a foul-smelling salve, laid the pad in the wound and taped the edges securely in place. "That'll allow some air to get to it while it heals. Rinse it out a couple of times a day and redress it with clean gauze. Come back if it begins to look or smell rotten." Then he fashioned another sling—this one properly done and comfortable. "Keep it as clean as you can, and come back if it starts to fester," the soldier reiterated as the two men thanked him and left.

Whitlaw led the way to a dry goods store that had re-opened for business and bought the Irishman the largest white cotton shirt they had in stock. Even so, it was none too big on Glasheen's massive shoulders and chest.

"What about the airplane?" Glasheen asked as they left the store.

"Could you help me push it to the house? We'll tie it down in the corner between the hedge and adobe wall where it'll have some protection from the wind. I'll put a canvas tarp over the motor and the cockpits. That'll have to do until I can figure out some more permanent arrangement."

With the help of two willing soldiers, it took them a half hour to roll the Jenny five hundred yards out of Camp Furlong, and across the road to the nearby adobe house.

Once the plane was secured, they broke for an early lunch since they'd had nothing to eat that day. Fried bacon sandwiches and canned soup made the meal. Whitlaw felt rather strange raiding the cupboard and using the same utensils Wil Scoggins had used a couple of days before. It seemed impossible that Wil was gone for good. "Concentrate on what's ahead," he muttered to himself. He threw a leg over the chair and sat down to eat at the rough wooden table.

"What's that y'say?" Glasheen asked, looking up from his food.

"Just an old man giving himself advice," Whitlaw answered, feeling a little embarrassed at this habit he'd picked up living alone these past months.

"Advice, is it? I could be usin' a little o' that m'self."

"Then here it is," Whitlaw said, putting his sandwich down on the plate. "Stay here until that wound heals and help me while I solo in that Jenny out there."

Glasheen's eyes widened in the ruddy face, and Whitlaw could hardly keep from laughing at the astonished look.

"Solo, y'say? And by that you're meaning to take off, fly around, and land that thing by yourself?"

"That's right."

"The silver threads in your topknot might be a sign you've seen a few summers."

"A goodly number."

"I've always been told that wisdom comes with age."

"Correct."

"Is it wise or sensible to try to imitate the hawks and vultures?"

"War and revolution and piloting an automobile at fifty miles an hour aren't sensible or wise, either, but men do them all the time. In fact, you're here to buy weapons to fight your own revolution . . . something an older, wiser man would avoid."

"You've got a point," Glasheen conceded. "Just living from day t'day is hazardous, as both of us have found out in the many years we've been walking on this earth. And we're not likely to get t' heaven in our present form."

"Now you're talking," Whitlaw said, spooning up his soup. "A prudent man takes calculated risks, and hopes for the best. Then, if the Lord still sees fit to take him. . . ."

"I'll be askin' ya for one favor, though."

"What's that?"

"Put me in your will before y'climb into that cockpit."

Chapter Six

"When I yell . . . 'switch off!' . . . pull the propeller through two or three times to prime the cylinders. Then I'll holler . . . 'contact!' You give her a spin and jump back," Whitlaw said, pulling on his leather gloves. "Just like I showed you."

For once, Glasheen was rather subdued, and he nodded without speaking.

Whitlaw stepped carefully up onto the trailing edge of the lower wing and swung a leg over the lip of the rear cockpit coaming. The view from the rear seat was definitely better than from the front, he thought, settling in and fastening the safety belt. Thank God these Jennies had been redesigned by the Curtiss engineers and improved since those earlier models that required the pilot to work the ailerons by leaning his body side to side in a shoulder harness with thin cables attached. That was akin to warping the wings as they did on the very early Wright brothers' heavier-than-air craft. At least now he had a wheel and two foot pedals.

He and Glasheen had positioned the plane facing into a very slight southerly breeze. The sun had just cleared the horizon on his left and he could see his breath in the March cold.

He had stayed awake late the night before, listing on a

pad everything he could recall of Wil Scoggins's instructions. Now he went over that checklist for take-off, referring to the pad sitting in his lap. He would keep the list handy until these actions became automatic from practice.

He pulled on the leather helmet and set the goggles in place, then buttoned the leather jacket to his chin. He worked the wheel back and forth and side to side to be sure the flaps were working properly. He had added two quarts of oil, then topped off the twenty-two gallon fuel tank from a steel drum of gasoline that Slocum had given him permission to use.

He leaned over the side of the cockpit. "After she's warmed up, I'll give you a signal to pull the chocks."

Glasheen waved an acknowledgment from out front.

For his solo attempt, Whitlaw had chosen a field a quarter mile south of the Camp Furlong parade ground. It was March 12th, two mornings after the raid. He wanted to get this over with before the camp was completely awake, before any more troops arrived, and before the wind picked up, as it was sure to do as the day warmed. And he wanted to get it over before he allowed himself any more time to think about it. If he cracked up on take-off, Glasheen was here to rescue him, or to run for help, or at least be a witness to what happened, if Whitlaw should not survive. The thought of hitting the ground with all that fuel out front made him cringe. He wasn't afraid of dying, but he'd always had a horror of burning to death.

He pulled the choke on, made sure the magneto switch was in the down position. "Switch off!" he yelled. He saw the propeller blade flip through three half turns. "Stand clear!" he yelled. He flipped the switch on, then took a deep breath and exhaled slowly. "Contact!"

The wooden propeller flipped through a half turn, but

nothing happened. Glasheen's curious face appeared from around the front of the fuselage.

"Again!" Whitlaw cried. "This time, swing your leg up and kick back to give yourself some leverage."

Glasheen's head disappeared. The propeller blade flipped, the motor caught, sputtered, then roared to life, blowing a cloud of white smoke from the exhausts, obscuring everything.

Whitlaw worked the throttle, then gradually eased the choke off as the engine settled down to a steady rumble. Over the last few months he'd developed an ear for the sound of this particular engine, and he could tell if all eight cylinders were firing properly. His judgment of its revolutions and performance was almost as accurate as a tachometer. He had a tach, an altimeter, and a fuel gauge, and that was it.

When the smoke cleared, he saw Glasheen standing well to the left of the plane, waiting for his next signal. Whitlaw fumbled inside the leather jacket for his pocket watch. He had to pull off his lined gloves to pop open the case. He would give the engine a good five minutes to warm up. No rushing. No cheating. On this cold morning, he had to be sure it was at its correct operating temperature before he began his take-off run, which meant the coolant in the radiator had to be just over 100 degrees. There would be no stalling out at a critical point because the engine was still cold when he gave it full power. Even at its best, this engine was none too powerful for what it was called on to do. He had read where the French had just introduced the Nieuport 17 into combat in Europe. It was the latest thing in a small, fast fighter, powered by a rotary engine. As he sat listening to the engine rumble, he almost wished he were hearing the power of a lighter rotary. But he'd read that rotary engines caused other problems for a pilot. The whole engine spun around the crankshaft, creating terrific gyroscopic force. A pilot had constantly to correct for the plane's tendency to pull to one side. On the ground, the pilot was often in the crapper as a result of ingesting a constant fine mist of castor oil thrown back by the prop blast. He grinned at the thought of what might happen if a pilot couldn't get down quick enough when the urge hit him.

Then the reality of his situation came hammering back to him, and all humor vanished. He had no intention of dying, but he was ready to join his late wife—if this should prove to be his last day alive. The thought of past decades flickered in front of his mind's eye like some black and white moving picture. For years he'd struggled to make a living, dealing with irate or stupid bosses during his long career with the railroad. He pictured his children in bed with scarlet fever or measles, then days when his train had been snowbound in blowing drifts. But there were good times, too—soft summer days when they had picnicked in the loess hills—all gone now as if they'd never happened. But he felt sure that credit for those days was stored up somewhere. He firmly believed that nothing was ever really lost. He was perfectly prepared to die today, except for one thing that still rankled, something that needed to be resolved before he could say—"It's finished."—the mystery of those damned rifles that he'd been accused of stealing. Even though he'd never been officially charged or prosecuted, the humiliation was still there. Maybe this was an injustice he'd have to suffer, as he had endured all other trials in his life.

He glanced at his watch. Six minutes. Time to go. He snapped the timepiece closed and tucked it into his pocket under the jacket. *Concentrate on everything Wil Scoggins told you about flying this thing,* he thought. *Were you really paying attention during his take-off drill?* Once aloft, he knew he could fly, but getting up and down was going to be tricky. He tried not to listen to Scoggins's spectral voice telling him he wasn't yet ready to solo. The lieutenant was just overly cautious. Whitlaw knew he had the skill; it was confidence he lacked. Now, he was about to gain it, or. . . .

He opened the throttle gradually, listening to the contented rumble increase to a full-throated roar, felt the cold air of the prop blast washing back over the windscreen, the whole craft vibrating like some giant animal straining to break loose from its leash.

He raised the flaps of his leather helmet and listened intently. The engine was running smoothly at maximum power. He dropped the ear flaps, and leaned out to give the signal to Glasheen. The stocky Irishman sprang in near the wing, grabbed a short rope, and yanked. Both chocks came flying out and he dashed back out of the way, dragging the wooden blocks by the rope.

The ungainly Jenny began its roll, bumping over the packed earth, slowly gaining speed. Whitlaw took a deep breath and tried to relax his grip on the wheel. He was bouncing a lot more than he'd expected. But he'd walked over every foot of this take-off run to be sure that no big rocks or ruts or cracks in the dry earth would trip him. On wetter airfields, unshielded wheels often threw up clods of mud that were flung forward, shattering wooden propellers. But not here, he thought, as a screen of dust was being blown up behind him.

"Hold the nose down . . . ," he muttered as the Jenny gained speed. "Not yet . . . not yet. . . . She's close to flying speed. Bring up the tail. Ready . . . just a few more seconds. . . ." He held his breath and pulled back on the wheel. The bouncing ceased as the Jenny became airborne. Too steep! She was stalling! He shoved the wheel forward to gain speed. Too much. The nose dropped and the wheels struck hard, bouncing the plane back up. A flatter angle this time. "Come on . . . come on . . . keep climbing. . . ." He gradually gained altitude. "Steady . . . steady . . . hold it right there." The Jenny responded beautifully. "Easy on the wheel," he muttered. "No sudden moves." How often had Scoggins told him to have a light touch on the controls?

He kept climbing, then finally threw a quick glance over the side. He was about a thousand feet up. He eased forward on the wheel and the plane leveled off. It was only then that he began to breathe normally again. The plane was heading south and he was probably already across the international boundary. Yes, there was the wire fence snaking along over the desert terrain far below. Time to turn back. He eased down on the throttle so the engine wasn't screaming at full power. Now for a nice gentle bank to the right. "Careful with the pedals. . . . Ahh . . . nicely done," he complimented himself, talking his way through the maneuvers, slowly relaxing as he gained confidence.

Columbus and Camp Furlong lay dead ahead. The men and women of the town were probably just getting up. They would have no idea of the momentous thing taking place over their very heads. An old, retired railroader with two bad shoulders was soaring over them like an eagle, defying the laws of gravity. He doubted if the Wright brothers, on their first flight at Kittyhawk, could have been more thrilled than he was at this moment. He felt light and free, no longer earth-bound. He roared his joy at the heavens, but the sound of his voice disappeared in the slipstream and the noise of the engine.

Several seconds later, he spotted Glasheen waving his arms in jubilation as the field approached, then passed beneath his wings. He flew over Columbus and about two miles farther. Then he tried a gentle bank to the left. Everything smooth. He was flying west now, the rising sun at his back creating elongated shadows of houses and scattered trees on the earth. He looked up and around. The sky was a deep blue, and cloudless. Another gorgeous day was in the making. He flew west for another ten minutes, dropping down to about seven hundred feet to follow the railroad. This was a familiar route. He and his instructor had flown this same course many times. Then he put the Jenny into a shallow dive, and banked around for the flight back. The sun was high enough now that it was not stabbing his eyes through the lenses of the goggles. It would provide plenty of light for landing—his next big hurdle.

He circled the field, seeing the soldiers of Camp Furlong staring up at him. Where was that windsock Scoggins had put up? Surely Colonel Slocum hadn't removed it already, since other planes were coming here. Yes, there it was. The breeze out of the south had picked up some, but was still light. He spotted Glasheen, standing to one side of the flight path. He flew north of town about a quarter mile, gave himself plenty of room to come around in a bank, line up the landing field, and gradually begin his descent. This time he was too cautious. When he was almost over the landing site, he realized he was far too high. He would go around and try again. On the second attempt, he went in on a steeper glide path, backing off on the throttle, braking with the flaps. When he was near touchdown, the ground seemed to rush up at him. He fought the panic that screamed at him to yank back on the wheel. He kept the nose steady. Now . . . down. He flared out and dropped the last several feet. But the Jenny hit too hard and bounced five feet into the air, then came down again, hard, but stayed down and he cut the engine to let the plane roll, losing speed. Surely the landing gear was built for such punishment. He would learn to taxi later, he thought, letting out a great sigh of relief. "Any landing where you don't break your airplane or yourself is a good landing," Scoggins had been fond of saying.

For several long seconds, after the propeller whipped to a stop and the plane stopped rolling, he sat and listened to the blessed silence. He was damp with perspiration under his jacket. He pulled off his helmet and goggles; the cool air felt good. "Well, Wil, you and I did it," he muttered. "It wasn't pretty, but now I've got the confidence I can do it again." He unbuckled his seat belt as Glasheen ran up.

"Congratulations!" he yelled, thrusting up his hand. Whitlaw gripped it over the cowling. "B'God, I didn't think to see you again this side o' the abyss."

Whitlaw grinned in spite of himself as he climbed somewhat stiffly out of the cockpit. "Sorry to disappoint you," he said.

"Oh, it's happy I am to see you back on the ground in one piece, although I wouldn't have given a farthing for your chances a time or two there."

"Before it gets too windy, help me push this plane back to the shelter of our cabin. I'd taxi up to the road, but I don't want to push my luck. This is enough for one day."

"How about some ham and eggs? I suddenly got my appetite back," Whitlaw said, securing the last knot on the canvas engine cover.

"B'God, I'm thinkin' you Yanks eat meat every meal. It's a habit I could get used to." Glasheen grinned.

"Don't you have meat in Ireland?"

"In my corner of the world, it's on the hoof. Mostly we sell the wool and ship the pigs to market. Now and again we have some mutton or bacon, but livestock is a cash crop, not generally for our table."

They started down the street toward the restaurant. Justin Potter, the gossipy hotel clerk, stopped on the street a short distance ahead of them, consulting his watch.

"Probably a good two hours till opening time," Whitlaw commented as they came up to Potter. Since he'd been suddenly thrown out of a job, Potter had been spending much time in the local pub, gathering and dispensing news and rumor; he made the most of his brief fame as an eyewitness to the murder of his hotel guests.

"Just the two I've been looking for," Potter said, brightening up as he put his watch away.

"Why's that?"

"The ashes have cooled down enough to get into the hotel safe. Nothing damaged."

"Let's go get our stuff."

The clerk led them back up the street where the clean-up of the destroyed buildings was under way. Men with bandannas tied across their noses and mouths shoveled débris and heaved burned timbers into wagons and two trucks. Fine ash was coating everything, downwind. A path had been shoveled to the big iron safe. Blackened and blistered, its gold lettering gone, it stood tall and indestructible in the surrounding devastation. Potter shielded the lock with his body to work the combination, then jerked the handle, and the door swung open easily. The heat had not touched anything inside, and Glasheen retrieved his letter of credit, a few gold coins and bills, his return tickets, and other small items he'd left for security in a handbag the night he'd checked in. Whitlaw took out a canvas bag he kept stashed, containing mostly just a few items of his wife's gold jewelry, a cameo brooch—things he'd given her over the years or she had inherited that he couldn't bring himself to part with. The bag also held the list of serial numbers on the stolen rifles.

Potter swung the safe door shut and turned the handle with a loud *click*. "They're having a funeral service this afternoon at the camp for the soldiers who were killed," he informed them over his shoulder as he spun the dial on the lock.

"Thanks. We'll be there," Whitlaw said as he and Glasheen started away.

The chaplain conducted a joint, open-air service on the parade ground at one o'clock. With the lack of cold storage and the distance from any major cities, it was decided to bury all the deceased soldiers at Camp Furlong, with appropriate military honors, pending any later disposition of the bodies by relatives.

The crowd included many townspeople. Whitlaw and Glasheen stood near the rear, listening to the eulogy over the heads of the crowd. A row of coffins stood side-by-side, fronting the speakers' platform. Whitlaw turned and looked to the east. A quarter mile away a section of disturbed soil marked the spot where a burial party had shoveled under the charred remains of the Mexican raiders. If lack of respect for the bodies of the enemy was any indication of feeling, then "hate" was too soft a word for the way the soldiers regarded Pancho Villa's men. These were brutal times, he reflected. And they weren't over yet.

When the chaplain finished speaking and the last, mournful notes of "Taps" had blown away on the breeze, the civilian crowd dispersed while the soldiers were dismissed company by company.

Whitlaw plucked a tiny, blue wildflower nearby that had

somehow survived the harsh climate and the tramping of many feet. He approached and placed the hardy little flower atop the rough wooden coffin that was marked with the name of Lieutenant Wilford Scoggins. Pausing a few seconds with his hat by his side and his hand on the box, he muttered: "We never know how or when, do we, Wil? Thanks for everything. Maybe I'll see you again someday." He blinked away the wetness in his eyes as he replaced his hat and moved away, thinking of all the friends and relatives he'd said good bye to over the years.

Whitlaw stopped at the bank to see the vice president, Clifford Rondell, the landlord of their little adobe house. Rondell seemed relieved to have a new renter and didn't even require any paperwork as they shook hands on the deal and Whitlaw paid a month's rent in advance.

The rest of that day he and Glasheen spent replacing the basic necessities that had been lost in the fire. A minimum of clothing—underwear, shirt, pants, belt, socks, handker-chiefs, along with razors, soap, towels, and a blanket each— they picked out at the general mercantile. A few groceries completed their buying. It would do for now, Whitlaw thought, as they stashed their purchases in the adobe. He wanted to go flying that afternoon, but the wind was gusting, as usual, and he dared not attempt it.

But for each of the next three mornings they were up before dawn and on the parade ground with the Jenny by daylight. He was eager to get in as much flying time as possible before the handful of pilots of the 1st Aero Squadron arrived by train with their disassembled aircraft. His pride would not allow him to look like a rookie pilot in front of these younger, more experienced aviators.

The early morning calm gave him time to practice take-offs and landings—nothing complicated aloft. Even though

Scoggins had demonstrated some aerobatic maneuvers, a roll, an inside loop, and how to recover from a spin, Whitlaw was taking this one step at a time. There would be opportunity for all that later, if necessary.

By the third morning, he had done several dozen touch-and-go take-offs and landings. He was becoming comfortable with those two vital aspects of flying. He practiced taxiing, certainly a trickier maneuver than driving an automobile, he guessed. At least the driver of a car could see where he was going. From the rear cockpit of a tail-dragger such as this, he could see out either side, but not directly forward. He could see ahead on the ground only during those critical seconds just before lift-off when he'd almost reached flying speed and brought the tail up to level the plane. Little by little, he became more at ease with the idiosyncrasies of the Jenny.

However, on the third morning, he was suddenly awakened to the hazards of overconfidence. He had practiced longer than usual, disregarding the rising wind as the desert began to warm up. As he was landing for the final time, a sudden gust of wind caught him from the side and tilted the Jenny up on one wheel. The left wing dipped and touched the hard earth. He was saved from disaster by the curved skid under the lower wing. It allowed him that vital second to regain control, bringing the plane to a stop without damage. For several long seconds he sat in the cockpit, his knees too weak to climb out. He felt the slight burning of bursitis in the muscles of his upper arm. Maybe this really was a young man's pursuit, he thought, but rejected that idea, since he knew his own reflexes were nearly as quick and sharp as they'd always been.

Glasheen came running up. "That was quite a trick . . . bouncing one wing like that."

For a moment, Whitlaw was tempted to let on that it was

intentional, but didn't have the heart for it. "It almost got away from me," he admitted in a strained voice as he struggled up out of his seat.

Glasheen nodded as if that's what he expected to hear, but didn't want to say it.

That afternoon, two special trains from El Paso arrived and disgorged several hundred troops and their gear. Cavalry horses clattered down the ramps from stock cars. The throng swept over Camp Furlong, resulting in massive, organized confusion. Sergeants yelled and cursed while tents were unloaded and erected amid clouds of dust. Kicking, braying pack mules worked off pent-up energy on being released from hours of confinement in stock cars.

The only reason Whitlaw's makeshift airfield was not overrun by the horde was because Major Lindsley directed it be roped off to reserve plenty of room for the imminent arrival of the 1st Aero Squadron.

Whitlaw watched in amazement. He had never witnessed a major military operation uncoiling. "If there's this much turmoil and confusion when they start after Villa, they'll wind up shooting each other," he remarked to Glasheen.

Columbus was awash in the effluvium of news, rumors, and gossip. Some of the civilians watched the operation from a safe distance, holding El Paso newspapers that had been tossed from the train in bundles and quickly sold on the street.

Headlines glimpsed, conversations overheard—it was as if they absorbed the details of the expedition by osmosis. President Wilson had ordered a punitive expedition across the border after Villa, and this was just the first wave of troops that were to assemble here from both East and West. General Pershing had selected the 7th, 10th, 11th, and 13th

Cavalry Regiments and the 6th and 16th Infantry Regiments. The numbers of the various units meant nothing to Whitlaw, but the soldiers here seemed to recognize these regiments as being composed of the most experienced regulars in the U.S. Army. Many of them had seen combat in the Philippines and all had spent months guarding the desert border. The Corps of Engineers was adding two companies. An ambulance and field hospital would travel, as well as a detachment of the Signal Corps who would attempt to keep their primitive radios operating.

There seemed to be some disagreement about the 6th Field Artillery. They were bringing along eight mountain howitzers—rifled cannon that could throw an exploding shell 5,500 yards. However, older heads among the officers at Camp Furlong questioned the wisdom of lugging a weapon that, disassembled, required four mules to carry it, plus ten more mules to haul the ammunition, plus the men and equipment to take care of the mules. All this might still have made sense, they argued, except for the fact that in the entire U.S. Army, there were fewer than 6,000 rounds for these guns—only several minutes' worth in a hot fight. And no rounds to spare for practice.

"Not too impressive, is he?" Whitlaw commented as he and Glasheen watched General John J. Pershing step down from a passenger coach of a westbound train the next morning, and return the salute of a Camp Furlong officer.

"He'd never make it in the French or Italian armies," Glasheen agreed.

"Olive drab from top to bottom. If he were a Mexican general, he'd be covered with gold braid, a lot of colorful trim, and a chest full of medals that he'd probably awarded himself."

The general strode toward the depot, the heels of his riding boots clumping hollowly on the platform. He wore the flared jodhpurs of the cavalry and a peaked, straight-brim campaign hat set squarely on his graying head. A lean, no-nonsense man, Whitlaw decided, as Pershing and his party passed the depot bench. The serious face was bisected by a brushy mustache just to the corners of his thin gash of a mouth. No smile creases lined the flat, weathered cheeks.

"British officers are often pig-headed and bulldog determined, but they come mostly from the genteel class." Glasheen jerked his head toward the retreating general. "This one has a hard look about him, like a pub brawler. I'd hate to have him after me. What might y'know of the man?"

They watched Pershing wave off the offer of a ride in the open staff car and continue walking toward the camp headquarters building two hundred yards away. A photographer ran ahead of the general and his coterie and made two or three attempts to get set and focused for a quick shot. He finally succeeded just as Pershing reached the road where Colonel Slocum and Major Lindsley came out to meet him.

"Well, I know his subordinates respect his leadership. He doesn't just give orders. I read in the paper some time ago he was recommended for the Congressional Medal of Honor for leading his men in a charge on some hill in the Philippines. But he withdrew his name. Said he'd done nothing more than the men around him had done. After some pressure, he finally accepted a lesser decoration." Whitlaw paused. "But I'd wager his grim look isn't due just to the assignment he's been given now."

"How so?"

"A few weeks after he was transferred to Texas, he got word that his wife and daughters had been killed in a fire in their wooden quarters in San Francisco's *presidio*."

"Awful!"

"Yeah. A servant managed to save his little son. I hear tell he throws himself into his work. Military duties are a distraction, an escape from the grief."

"Then I'd say this bandit, Pancho Villa, has a lot t'worry about."

"Look at the size of this expedition," Whitlaw said, waving an arm at the dust cloud being stirred up at the camp a quarter mile away. "And Potter, who seems to know everything, says this is only about half of it. The rest of the troops are assembling at Culberson's ranch, fifty miles southwest of here. Pershing will lead that column himself. There will be close to five thousand men and over four thousand animals in two columns, trying to flank Villa and head him off. Can you imagine such a force after one man and a few hundred of his ragged followers? It's like sending an elephant to tromp on a hornets' nest."

"As we found out the other night, hornets can move faster and they can sting," Glasheen muttered thoughtfully.

The punitive expedition entered Mexico in two columns, about twelve hours and fifty miles apart. Just after noon on March 15th, Major Frank Tompkins of the 13th Cavalry led the first column from Columbus straight south toward the border. They made no effort to conceal the fact that this large force was entering a foreign country. In fact, the Mexican troops at the border and at the dusty little adobe town of Palomas, just across the line, had departed sometime earlier, leaving only an aged couple behind to see the advancing Americans.

Again Whitlaw and Glasheen were spectators, along with most of the townspeople, as the middle-aged major, astride his sorrel, swung his arm forward and the cavalry column began to move, followed slowly by the infantry. Then came several heavy trucks, whining in low gear as they strained to pull their canvas-covered loads, pneumatic and hard rubber tires churning up still more dust. The breeze obscured everything in a pale brown haze. Two wagon companies followed with 27 wagons, 112 mules, 6 horses, and three dozen men each. It looked to Whitlaw like some giant, green and brown python, uncoiling and slithering away ever so slowly into the southern desert.

Two hours later the parade was over and the column only a lingering dust cloud far to the south. The crowd of townspeople broke up and went about their business, satisfied swift retribution for the brutal attack on their town was at hand.

Possibly because he was already several miles closer to their objective, Casas Grandes, Pershing delayed the departure of his column from Culbertson's ranch until the stroke of midnight. By giving the Columbus column a head start, perhaps he hoped to rendezvous at nearly the same time.

From the map published in the El Paso newspaper, the troops would be following a long, flat, featureless valley for the first hundred miles or more. This valley generally flanked the eastern side of the towering Sierra Madre mountain chain that thrust its rugged spine into the sky like the ribbed back of a giant lizard. The newspaper could only speculate what General Pershing might do once the troops reached their first objective, the Mormon settlement of Colonia Dublan, just above the Mexican village of Casas Grandes.

The 1st Aero Squadron had arrived the day before, almost unnoticed among the throngs of men, animals, and equipment. But Whitlaw had seen the ten pilots, the one civilian mechanic, and some eighty enlisted men traveling together.

They had unloaded the Jennies from the freight cars, then uncrated and assembled them on a portion of the parade ground, roped off for the purpose. In contrast to the much larger operation, the Aero Squadron seemed disciplined and organized, and had the planes assembled in the better part of a day. After the huge column marched and rode south, Whitlaw wandered over to take a look at the aviators and their Jennies. His first impression was that these pilots seemed impossibly young—barely out of their teens. The only one of them who seemed old enough to grow a decent mustache was Lieutenant Foulois. He looked to be about forty. Clear-eyed, he moved with a self-assured fluidity as he inspected the planes that were beginning to reappear in their correct configurations from the crates. Whitlaw paused at the edge of the rope barricade. Should he go on in and meet this leader of the 1st Aero Squadron and explain that he was a fellow pilot and had a Jenny parked not far away?

"I wouldn't be for puttin' m'self in the way of ridicule," was Glasheen's response when Whitlaw mentioned his intention.

Lieutenant Scoggins had accepted him as an equal in all things, but Glasheen's remark suddenly brought Whitlaw the realization that he was about a generation removed from even Foulois, the oldest man in the squadron. Silently accepting Glasheen's assessment, Whitlaw only stood watching with several other civilians at the rope barricade for a half hour, then turned away. "Ready for some supper?" he asked.

The next morning, Foulois ordered two planes to make a test flight of thirty miles straight south and return. If his squadron was to function as swift messengers between scattered units and to provide reconnaissance, he had to be sure his aircraft were functioning properly.

Whitlaw was at the camp hospital having Glasheen's dressing changed when the two Jennies, their engines wide-open, cleared the parade ground, one after another and slowly droned out of sight in the clear sky.

They were in the saloon sipping beer, an hour later, when the planes returned and landed. At the time Whitlaw didn't know the purpose of the flight, but shortly Potter came in and announced to one and all that: "Those motorized kites don't have much horsepower. But that valley's only about four thousand three hundred feet elevation."

Whitlaw had never considered the limitation that height above sea level would have on the performance of an engine—just as percentage of grade affected what weight a steam locomotive could pull. The laws of physics were inexorable.

Chapter Seven

"Come and take a short flight with me," Whitlaw suggested casually. "We'll go west a few miles and be back in an hour or two."

"Are y'daft, man? I'm not as stupid as I look, y'know."

"You entrusted yourself to a ship on the ocean for many days."

"It's not the length of the trip that bothers me. Besides, ships have been around a lot longer than airplanes."

Whitlaw shook his head. "For a man desperate enough to cross the sea to find weapons to fight a deadly revolution, and then survives an attack by Mexican bandits, you've suddenly gone very conservative."

"If I'm going to throw my life away, I want it to be for a cause I believe in. When a man has the fire of youth pulsing in his blood, he's reckless because he thinks he's going to live forever. It's the nature of things. The older one gets, the more he realizes what a precious and precarious thing life really is, and begins to use his remaining time a lot wiser."

"I'm older than you, and I don't think that way."

"You strike me as an eternal optimist."

"I just have confidence in my ability and my knowledge of what that plane will do."

"No one has control over the unexpected. A little fear is a

good thing. It has kept me alive and healthy into my fifties."

Whitlaw said nothing for a minute as he poured himself another cup of coffee to go with the fresh slice of bread and jam. He had just returned from an early hike to Camp Furlong to meet Lieutenant Foulois. The squadron leader had shaken his hand, looked him up and down, and remarked predictably: "Aren't you a little old to be taking up flying?"

Whitlaw had anticipated the question. "They didn't have planes when I was your age."

"Good answer," the lieutenant nodded. "Age is a state of mind, as the old cliché goes. It's true for a pilot, too, as long as he still has the co-ordination and eyesight to go with a positive state of mind."

Whitlaw had purposely tucked his bifocals into his shirt pocket before he'd introduced himself. The leader of the 1st Aero Squadron was a little out of focus.

"I won't take up any more of your time, Lieutenant. I just wanted to meet you and say I have a Jenny here and available for use, if you should need it for anything . . . besides spare parts." He grinned. "I come with the plane, and will be happy to assist you and your men with any flying chores."

"Thanks, Whitlaw. I'll keep you in mind. In this business, you never know when or where you can use a little assistance. As you can see, we're a mighty small outfit. Likely to need all the help we can get. One more plane and pilot would increase our strength by more than ten percent."

"Never thought of it that way. I live in that adobe just across the road if you need to get hold of me."

"Thanks. I'll remember that. It won't be long before we see action. General Pershing will need some quick communications and reconnaissance in a day or two when he gets a good way south and begins to deploy his units."

Whitlaw wondered if the dashing aviator was just trying to humor an old man. "By the way, Lieutenant Wilford Scoggins, who was one of the men who died in that raid, taught me to fly. That was his plane he flew on his off-duty hours. I'm sure he would have asked for a transfer to your squadron had he lived."

"Sorry, I never knew him."

They parted with another handshake, and Whitlaw returned to the adobe for breakfast and to try a little persuasion on Glasheen. It would be different. He lounged back next to the window in a shaft of warm sunshine. The jam was excellent—sold by a local housewife who made it from the fruit of the prickly pear cactus.

"You know, I'll be flying along the railroad. Before Scoggins died, he and I thought maybe we could scout for some clue about those missing rifles," he said, taking a sip of the steaming coffee. "I could really use another pair of eyes."

Glasheen looked up, distractedly rubbing the lower part of his wounded arm still in the sling. He chewed thoughtfully at the corner of his mustache. "Well . . . since you put it that way . . . ," he said finally, "maybe I could take a chance."

"Sure. Put yourself in the hands of Divine Providence."

"B'God, I'm thinkin' Providence might not extend to places where only m'guardian angel can fly." He sighed deeply. "The things I do for m'country!" Glancing toward the window, he asked: "How bad is the wind out there today?"

"Very light for a change. That's why I proposed this. Air's getting muggy. Clouds moving in from the west. Wouldn't be surprised to see a little rain by nightfall. We could sure use it," he added.

"Well. . . ." Glasheen flexed his injured arm. "I need to

rest m'shoulder and let my guardian angel go off duty for a while. But . . . against my more mature judgment, I'll go. Just this once, mind ye," he added sharply as Whitlaw couldn't suppress a grin. "After all, it's the reason I made this long trip to America in the first place. As long as I'm here, I might as well see what I can do to help find those missing guns. At least I can report back that I did every-thing I could . . . including risking m'life."

"That's the spirit!"

Glasheen looked glum.

"That wound should be a lot better by now. It's been ten days since you were shot."

"It's pretty deep, but the gash is filling in. I'd best go have the dressing changed, now that I think about it. When are we taking off?"

"As soon as you get back, we'll gas up and get going."

They taxied to the end of the parade ground at half past one that afternoon, swung into position, and, with the eight-cylinder engine roaring at full throttle, went into their take-off roll. They lifted off into a light crosswind and began to climb. Whitlaw, watching the grizzled head in the forward cockpit, felt an extra responsibility and was very careful to do everything just right. It wasn't as if he was careless when he was alone, but the weight of another life in his hands somehow made him more cautious.

When he leveled off at a thousand feet, he relaxed and noticed his unwilling passenger still gripping the padded edges of the cowling as if afraid he would be sucked out of the open cockpit by the rushing slipstream. All Whitlaw could see was the back of Glasheen's head, the goggle strap keeping some of his hair from whipping around. If Whitlaw had been able to communicate by voice, perhaps he could have calmed the Irishman's nerves.

He turned his attention back to flying. He had taken off in a southerly direction and could see the wire border fence ahead and, just beyond, the dusty little adobe village of Palomas. Time to change course. He used the pedal to give some gentle right rudder and turned the wheel. The bank was not steep, but Whitlaw grinned when his passenger reacted as if he were about to be dumped out. *With his lap belt secured, I could roll this thing over and he wouldn't fall out,* he thought. He then recalled his first reaction to the heeling of a sailboat and was more sympathetic.

He picked up the El Paso & Southwestern tracks and nudged the wheel forward, putting the Jenny into a shallow dive, leveling off at five hundred feet.

As they flew westward, he wondered what he should name his plane. He couldn't keep calling it "the Jenny". After all, it was the same model aircraft as the others here now. The only difference was the color and the fact that the military craft had numbers painted on their sides, such as 43 and 53, and a single star on the top of the rudder at the tail. But did people christen planes as they did ships? He didn't know. Perhaps not. But airplanes were still too new to have any such traditions established. He would broach the subject to Glasheen when they landed—if he could pry the Irishman's fingers loose from the cockpit.

Following the rails, he wondered how to get Glasheen to watch carefully as they flew along at seventy-five miles an hour. As rigid as his passenger appeared, Whitlaw thought the Irishman might just lose his breakfast if induced to look over the side at the desert. And that would not be good when sitting a few feet behind Glasheen.

After several minutes of flying level at low altitude, Glasheen twisted in his seat and looked back, his eyes wide behind the goggles. Whitlaw motioned by shading his eyes and looking over the side, and then pointing at Glasheen. The Irishman nodded that he understood, and began scanning the barren terrain below.

Even though the early afternoon sun was just ahead of them, it was obscured by a haze and didn't bother their eyes. Low, dark clouds were forming ahead on the horizon and quickly moving toward them. Or else their own speed made it seem that way. Just what Whitlaw hoped to see from the air that investigators had not seen from the ground two years ago, he wasn't quite sure. Maybe nothing. If a clue to the disappearance of those rifles lay along this stretch of tracks, surely the authorities would have found it long before now.

Whitlaw edged the Jenny to the left, so he and Glasheen could both look down to the right at the tracks without straining their necks. Holding the plane straight and level with a minimum of attention, he let his gaze drift along the terrain below, but saw nothing out of the ordinary. Nor did he really expect to. The tracks continued almost straight west with no sidings. A water tower passed beneath them, and the tracks continued through scattered desert scrub. The trainload of surplus weapons was last seen rolling through Columbus at 10 p.m. The stationmaster at Hachita had been at home, but claimed to have had a witness that saw the train pass there between 11 and 11:30 the same night. The authorities had concentrated their search on the seventy-mile stretch of isolated track between Columbus, Hachita, and Animas. Along that stretch there were three, widely-separated sidings by cattle-loading chutes. The only spurs were a sidetrack that ran sixty miles south from Hachita to Antelope Wells, on the border, and another that stretched forty miles south to the border from the tiny town of Animas.

109

Whitlaw stared ahead. The tracks curved to the north to pass through a low saddle between brown desert mountains. He eased back on the wheel and climbed to about 1,500 feet to get a better look ahead to see how far the next town was. But it was not yet in sight on the hazy horizon. He fumbled inside his jacket for his watch. It was easy to lose track of time up here, he'd discovered when flying with Scoggins. He popped open the case with his free hand. They'd been aloft for thirty-five minutes. Yes, that was about right. There was a mountain off to the right they'd used for a landmark. This was where they usually turned to fly back to Columbus. Today he would continue on. He had topped off the twenty-two gallon tank, and estimated it was good for two more hours. With storm clouds building and coming toward them, he figured to have a tailwind going home. They were approaching low desert mountains, the Cedar Mountains. If they kept heading to the northwest, they would encounter the Pyramid Mountains. South of that range, he remembered, lay a string called the Animas Mountains, the tallest peak of which was over 8,000 feet. He never claimed to be a geographer, but guessed all these smaller mountain ranges were only spurs of the much larger Mexican Sierra Madre. On a broader scale, if he could take this airplane up many miles above the earth, the Sierra Madre were only part of the vast ridge stretching from Alaska down to the tip of South America. Everything appeared larger at close range, so humans had divided these clumps of mountains, giving them many different names—the Rocky Mountains, the Sierra Madre, the Andes, and so on.

His reverie was interrupted by Glasheen who was emphatically gesturing at something below. Whitlaw glanced over the side. At first he saw nothing, and the noise of the engine and prop blast made questions impossible. He shook his head, indicating he didn't understand. Then he looked again. Still he noticed only the single track sweeping in a long, right-hand curve between the brown mountains. He held the plane steady and stared hard once more. The only thing that caught his attention was the faint trace of what appeared to be a spur track leading off toward the mountains. But there was no track. The only way he could discern any difference was by faint scratchings and a slightly lighter shade of soil. He was wearing his bifocals under his goggles, and squinted to see if that might sharpen his focus. But the lower halves of the bifocals got in the way and blurred out the image of the terrain.

"Damn these cheaters!" he swore in frustration, all the time knowing they were indispensable if he were to fly at all. He watched Glasheen still studying something below. He'd have to wait until later to find out what had drawn Glasheen's attention. For now he had to deal with the dark, thickening clouds looming up ahead. Although he could hardly feel it, the Jenny must have picked up a headwind because their speed over the ground had definitely decreased. The headwind was blowing the storm clouds directly toward them. He put the plane into a shallow dive and brought them down a 1,000 feet. Watching the ground, he could tell they had slowed perceptibly. He couldn't feel the actual wind, but knew it was retarding their progress, burning up fuel faster than he anticipated. How to estimate the use of the gasoline? This had never come up before. He and Scoggins had never been up long enough at a stretch, or run into adverse winds, to concern themselves with fuel economy. The vibrations and sloshing of the fuel in the tank caused the fuel gauge—a circular dial with a needle activated by a float in the tank—to be wildly inaccurate.

He felt a moment of panic, but quickly suppressed it. If necessary, he could set the Jenny down in the flat desert below, and they could flag down the next eastbound train. But how would he face Lieutenant Foulois after presenting himself as a competent pilot? It was too embarrassing to contemplate. An emergency landing because he ran out of fuel would certainly shake Glasheen's confidence in him. If the engine quit, could he glide in safely without power? He'd have to put it down before he ran completely out of gas. What of the surface? From several hundred feet up, it looked flat and smooth with only a few desert shrubs. But he knew it was likely grooved with tiny arroyos from erosion, split with numerous cracks from drought, and littered with small rocks and rodent holes that could spell disaster for a plane.

He tried to calculate in his head the probable speed of the headwind, estimate how fast he was going, how much they were being slowed, how fast the Jenny was burning fuel. It was all just dead reckoning, an estimate, a wild guess; there were no real figures to work with. The only thing he was sure of was how long they had been airborne. Holding the wheel with one hand, he consulted his watch. An hour and twenty minutes. He slid it back into his pocket and looked over the side. As low as they were, he should have felt a sensation of speed, but they seemed to be crawling along. Could a plane come to a complete standstill and stay in the air if the wind were strong enough? He had seen it happen to birds in strong winds, had even seen them blown backwards. What a strange notion—flying, but going nowhere.

While these thoughts were flashing through his mind, his hands and eyes automatically adjusted for the gusts that were beginning to push him northwesterly, toward the mountains. He scanned the thunderhead that now covered half the sky ahead, then flicked his eyes to the jiggling needle on the gas gauge. In spite of the wild gyrations of the pointer, he could tell the level was dropping precipitously. He couldn't get back to Columbus now, even with a tail wind. Whatever he decided, he couldn't allow himself to communicate his fear and uncertainty to Glasheen. And the decision had to be now. As a railroad conductor, he had had more time to weigh possibilities and make decisions. But the speed of flight precluded such leisurely ponderings. The ideal pilot would be a young man with an old aviator's experience. He now realized why Scoggins had been so deliberate about training him to meet all the contingencies before turning him loose to solo.

His frozen thought processes thawed enough for a solution to suggest itself. Relief flooded over him and he actually grinned just as Glasheen turned his worried face back toward him and pointed at the storm clouds ahead. Why hadn't he thought of it before? The town of Hachita couldn't be more than a few miles ahead. He banked left and took a good look. Sure enough, he saw a small town in the distance. It didn't matter what town. Dirt roads leading in and out of it would suit for a landing. And he would be near a source of gasoline. Horses, buggies, and autos would have to be warned off, but that shouldn't be a problem. Rutted and rough as the roads probably were, they had to be better than attempting a landing in the desert.

Lightning split the black mass of clouds and he caught his breath. The storm was rearing above and around them. What would hail and lightning do to this fragile plane, not to mention the terrific winds the storm contained?

The steady drone of the V-8 engine coughed, missed a beat, then surged on. He thought his heart had stopped. He

113

took a deep breath, his pulse began to race, and he was hardly aware of Glasheen's anguished look from the front seat. The gas gauge needle barely flickered above zero. Too late he wished he had climbed to give himself some altitude to glide if the motor quit. He was only about four hundred feet off the ground—too low to reach the town. He felt the wind begin to buck and twist the plane, and looked desperately for the dirt road. *There! Maybe two miles away, just off to the right.* He carefully banked around and headed for it. The first cold raindrops struck his face like thrown gravel. His goggles were blurring up with streaking rain water.

He lined up the Jenny with the road leading toward the small settlement—directly into the wind. No time to consider anything; he had to get it on the ground. One lone truck was heading out into the countryside, directly into his landing path! *Damn!* He would have to cut it close. If the driver would just see him and stop!

Whitlaw pushed the wheel forward and nosed the Jenny down, fighting to correct for the buffeting they were taking. The engine stumbled again, but the forward tilt of the craft must have drained the last little gasoline to the engine. It roared to life once more just as the ground was rushing upward. He flared out, and a sudden downdraft pancaked them down into a hard three-point landing. The plane bounced, but then the wind became a net, bringing them to a quick stop, only a few yards from the farm truck. The engine coughed and died. He flipped off the ignition.

"Hey, mister, you want to put that thing in my barn?" a man yelled. "She's gonna come a ripsnorter in a few minutes."

The voice came from the driver who had stopped his truck just in time. He seemed not at all surprised by the sudden appearance of an airplane on this road.

"Great!" Whitlaw yelled back.

"Here, I'll give 'er a tow," the farmer said, jumping out and grabbing a coil of rope from the back of the truck. "My barn's just over yonder about a quarter mile. It'll be safe there."

Chapter Eight

"I need a drink in honor of Saint Paddy," Glasheen said, raising his voice to make himself heard above the roar of rain pounding on the tin roof of the barn.

"What?" Whitlaw was squatting by the lower wing, examining the landing gear for possible damage from the hard landing.

"This is the Seventeenth, isn't it? Saint Paddy's day?"

"Either the Sixteen or Seventeenth. I've lost track," Whitlaw replied absently. "That happens when you're retired," he added with a grin as he straightened up.

"Well, if it isn't the right day, then I need it worse than the good saint for m'own jangled nerves," Glasheen said in a slightly shaky voice.

He looked decidedly wretched—wet, shivering, hair plastered to his forehead, whisker stubble showing salt and pepper against his pale cheeks. He seemed to be favoring his wounded arm, even though he no longer carried it in a sling.

Miserable as the Irishman appeared, at least he was alive. They both were. Less than twenty minutes ago that was all Whitlaw could have hoped for. Even the plane had suffered no obvious damage. If he continued to defy gravity, his lucky streak might run out someday, but it would not be today. He would have to develop a fatalistic attitude.

The farmer who had generously towed them to his barn had not even introduced himself. He'd just climbed into his truck, turned, and headed back to town. Either the storm had changed his mind about going on down the muddy road, or he had wanted to be the first to spread the word of their arrival.

"As soon as it lets up, we'll hike into town," Whitlaw said, moving back to avoid the spray that was being blown in through the open double doors.

Two hours later, in town, Whitlaw and Glasheen entered the hardware store and discovered the rancher had spread the word of their presence.

To catch as much of the trade as possible in this small town, store owner, Barney Mintor, had added a machine shop and garage.

"What do ya need?" he greeted them. "I can do most any kind o' mechanic work, from fixin' spring axles on buggies to repairin' automobile motors. If your aeroplane don't need any complicated parts, I can probably fix it."

"Nothing like that. Just ran out of gas," Whitlaw said.

"We got plenty," Minton replied, leading them out the front door. As an added incentive to the growing number of auto drivers, he had installed a gas pump out front that drew from a large storage tank at the side of the building.

"Don't appear the automobile is going to be just a passing fancy or a toy for the rich, thanks to Mister Ford," the lean Mintor remarked. "And now two aviators come in to gas up their flying machine. A flying machine . . . in Hachita!"

Whitlaw noticed the hardware even stocked work shirts and overalls. "Give me the largest shirt you've got . . . maybe one of those green plaid ones," he said, as he paid for twenty gallons of gasoline.

"Here, get out of that wet shirt and put this on, before you catch your death of cold," he said to Glasheen, tossing him the flannel shirt.

"Three fingers of poteen would start a blaze in m'blood," Glasheen muttered, peeling off the wet white shirt, and slipping into the new one.

"I need to keep my five-gallon cans," Mintor said, "but I'll have Roscoe deliver the gas out to your plane whenever you're ready." He went behind the counter and rang up the sale on a big, brass cash register, handing Whitlaw his change.

"If you're buying the shirt on m'back, then I'm buying the drinks," Glasheen said, flexing his shoulders in the shirt that was none too big on him. He had stopped shaking from the cold of the sudden drenching, and his nerves seemed under control. The brisk walk to town had probably helped warm him.

"I saw a saloon half a block from here," Whitlaw said, pushing open the door. "We need to talk."

Whitlaw eschewed the use of hard liquor, but loved his beer, and, twenty minutes later, the heavy, dark brew he sipped was just what he needed. Glasheen, used to the stronger stuff, had thrown back a shot of Jack Daniels and was sipping on a second.

Whitlaw took a long swallow of his beer and wiped his mouth with the back of his hand. "OK, tell me what it was you saw from the plane."

"You didn't notice it? 'Twas as plain as the nose on a hog," he said. "The spur that branched off from the main line near the mountains."

"There wasn't any spur that I saw."

"It's not there now . . . it *had* been, at some time or other."

"Oh, yes. I saw faint traces of something. Probably visible only from the air."

"When was it taken up?" Glasheen asked.

"I really don't know. I've read nearly everything of significance found during the investigation and don't recall any mention of a spur line along that stretch of track. I really think the authorities are convinced the train went south from Hachita and was run into Mexico."

They were silent for several seconds while they sipped their drinks. Besides the bartender, only one other mid-afternoon customer was in the place. Whitlaw and Glasheen sat at a small table by the front window where they could see the rain moving off to the east. The storm clouds were breaking, alternating sunlight with shadow. Puddles stood in the nearly deserted street. He hoped the air was warming. In the low desert, flowers would be in full bloom by this time in mid-March. Maybe the altitude here was too high for that.

"Did your bosses question ye at the time?" Glasheen asked.

"Yes. But mostly about my actions as a dispatcher. Only once did they ask me if I'd ever been to southern New Mexico. At that time I hadn't, and told them I was not familiar with the El Paso and Southwestern right of way."

"Why don't we look up the stationmaster here and have a chat with him?" Glasheen suggested, downing the last swallow of his whiskey. "I'm in no hurry to fly back. In fact, I've a good notion to take the train to Columbus."

"Coward." Whitlaw could hardly suppress a grin as they got up to leave and Glasheen dropped a coin as tip in the glass jar on the bar.

"I'd like to speak to Jeffrey Harnish," Whitlaw said to the man behind the barred ticket window at the Hachita depot.

"I'm Harnish," the man replied, stepping out from the cage and removing his green eye shade. "Come in. What can I do for you?" Evidently reacting to their surprise, Harnish, leading them into his office off the waiting room, continued: "I'm stationmaster and also function as ticket agent, porter, and telegrapher. The company figured to save money since there was very little business here. But they put on extra trains lately to bring in all those troops, and I was swamped. Things just slacked off since the expedition got under way. You caught me at a good time." He motioned them to two straight chains, then sat down in a wooden swivel chair behind his cluttered desk.

Whitlaw briefly introduced himself and Glasheen, then said: "I won't take up much of your time. I'm retired from the UP and live in Columbus. I'm curious about that shipment of Krag-Jorgensen rifles that disappeared around here two years ago."

"Whitlaw . . . yes, that rings a bell. I think I remember seeing your name in the paper in connection with that."

"Well, I have a few questions I'd like to ask you," Whitlaw hurried on before Harnish could recall that Whitlaw had been informally accused in the press.

"I've been through all that with the railroad detectives and the insurance people at the time," he said, raking a hand through his thinning hair a little nervously.

"Do you have any idea at all what happened to that train?"

"None," he said quickly. "All I know is that I was at home asleep when it passed through here at eleven ten that night."

"That's it?"

"That's it. Not a trace, after that."

"How do you know it passed through here if you were

off duty? A night watchman?"

"It was a special run, and had no need to stop here. Albert McSorley told the sheriff he saw it pass through."

"Isn't McSorley the town drunk?" Whitlaw asked.

"He has that reputation. But he was the only witness. This town packs it in and goes to bed by ten. Not much night life. McSorley said he was sleeping in the doorway of the depot when the train woke him as it went by."

"How do you know McSorley wasn't referring to the regular train that runs from El Paso and gets to Columbus about midnight?"

Harnish shrugged. "He might have been. Time doesn't mean much to poor old McSorley. He drinks to make it pass faster. For lack of any other witnesses, the investigators questioned him pretty close, but that's all they could get out of him. It was McSorley or nobody."

"And . . . ?"

"Nothing. Not a trace from that night to this. Vanished off the face of the earth. Strangest thing I ever experienced."

Whitlaw tried to read the expression of the middle-aged stationmaster who was regarding him, wide-eyed, over his half glasses. "You and I both know that it's physically impossible for an entire train to disappear. It had to go *somewhere.*"

"It may be physically impossible, but who's to say there aren't other forces at work in the universe?" Harnish hinted, waving his hands at the air around him. "This desert is big and empty."

"I suppose you're sayin' the wee folk could have carried it off to the fens," Glasheen commented.

Harnish glanced at the Irishman without changing his blank expression. "I'm not saying anything, because I don't know. If you've got some other explanation, I'd like to hear it," he added somewhat defensively.

"That's what I was hoping to get from you," Whitlaw said. "The Mexican revolution had been going on for nearly four years at the time those rifles vanished. Do you think there's any connection?"

"Who can say? There's a spur track on the edge of town here that runs off toward Antelope Wells on the border. And another that goes south from Animas, the next town west." He shrugged. "I've spent many a sleepless night trying to puzzle this out," he said finally. "But, when I'm on duty here, I'm so damned busy, I don't have time to notice much of anything. Something could have happened right under my nose, and I wouldn't have seen it. Off duty, I'm home with my wife, eating supper and relaxing. This job keeps me hopping. The company makes sure they get their money's worth out of me. I'm lucky if I can get up a poker game with a few friends every couple of weeks."

Whitlaw realized there was nothing further to be gained by talking with this man.

The telegraph key began to rattle, and Harnish sat up in his chair and grabbed a pencil. " 'Scuse me, gents."

Whitlaw rose and waved a good bye as Harnish began scribbling on a pad.

"That wasn't much help," Whitlaw said when the two men were outside on the depot platform.

"Do y'think the man was lyin'?" Glasheen paused to wring a few more drops of water out of the white shirt he was still carrying.

"If he was, he's very good at it."

"Aye, 'tis a strange world we live in, where nothing is as it seems."

"Nothing stranger than the disappearance of those guns."

"And him pretendin' to believe it was the fairies!" Glasheen snorted.

"Pretending?"

Glasheen nodded. "People who really have faith in magic and the existence o' the wee folk have a certain look about 'em. They're not generally the ones who work at practical jobs, like stationmaster. In my experience, those who are into the occult or the supernatural tend to be either completely uneducated, or are bookish and have their heads filled with the nonsense of past legends and folk tales, the works of alchemists, and the like."

"I'll take your word for it," Whitlaw said. "I can't detect anything that subtle."

"B'God, the man either has a glib tongue, or he really doesn't know anything," Glasheen said.

"Seems odd he wouldn't be more curious about it, though," Whitlaw said.

"It was worth a try, anyway," Glasheen said. "I suppose the investigators checked those two spurs he referred to that run south toward the border over west a ways."

"Pretty thoroughly," Whitlaw nodded. He took a deep breath. "Well, let's go tell that hardware man we're ready to gas up the plane before it gets to be supper time." Whitlaw took out his watch and began to wind it. "After I get the Jenny secured at home, I think maybe you and I should ride the cars back to where that spur used to be. Take a closer look. It probably won't tell us anything, but I don't know what else to do at this point. Maybe I can find out from the railroad people in El Paso if that spur was there two years ago, what it was used for, and when it was taken up."

"If it's all the same t'you, I believe I'll spend the night at the depot hotel and catch the morning train back," Glasheen said. "Might gentle m'nerves a bit."

Chapter Nine

"I didn't spot it," Glasheen said, stepping off the train.

"Spot what?" Whitlaw asked.

"What we thought was the spur track that wasn't there. I knew about where to look but, for the life of me, couldn't detect any trace of it from the train this morning."

Whitlaw's mind was churning as the pair left the platform and started toward their adobe. "If the spur wasn't there two years ago when the investigators did their search, and it can't be seen from ground level, no wonder it wasn't mentioned in the report."

"B'God, it makes no difference," Glasheen said. "If it's not there, it's not there. What we thought we saw didn't have anything to do with the train's disappearance. We're running around chasing our tails."

"What if a spur did exist and the train was run onto it and stolen?"

"Then where did it go? The traces I saw seemed to run directly toward that low mountain range. And was the track then snatched up behind it? No. . . ." The Irishman shook his head. "It smacks of some fantastic plot that's much too complicated for reality. There has to be a simpler explanation."

"The El Paso and Southwestern Railroad officials would know if a spur had split off there and when and why it was removed," Whitlaw said. "But if we go to their office in El

Paso and start asking questions, it could alert whoever in that company might have been in on it."

The stocky Irishman stopped in the dusty street and gave him a surprised look. "Y'think 'twas an inside job, then?"

"I do. A simple train robbery could be pulled off by any gang of outlaws, but to make a whole train disappear would take some inside knowledge and planning."

"So, what do y'suggest we do now?"

"Get a little camping gear together, borrow a hand car, and go out there ourselves and take our time to do some careful looking."

Glasheen cocked a brow at him. "And why do y'think the railroad will be makin' ye the loan of one o' their hand cars to be galavantin' out onto their main line?"

Whitlaw gave him a tight smile. "Never underestimate an old railroad man."

Whitlaw was in the process of filling a gallon jug with coal oil from the large tank on the side of the adobe house when he spied Justin Potter coming along the street. Whitlaw paused when he recognized the look of anticipation on the dapper little clerk's face. Potter had news he was bursting to tell.

"Well, you're the first to know," Potter said, coming up and removing his hat so he could wipe his brow with a white handkerchief.

"And what might that be?"

"I've just come from Camp Furlong." Potter paused and looked intently at Whitlaw as if trying to remember something. "Were you here yesterday?"

"No."

"I thought not. Then you didn't know that General Pershing sent orders by telegraph to have Lieutenant

Foulois and his squadron join him right away."

"Yes?" He corked the jug and waited for whatever news was coming.

"Lieutenant Foulois figured that the orders meant to report *immediately*. So he had his pilots climb into those Jennies and take off just before sunset."

"Flying at night into unfamiliar territory?" Whitlaw was astounded. He waited for more.

"It turned into a fiasco. No landmarks, no lights. There was supposed to be a big bonfire at Casas Grandes to mark their landing site. Following one another, they all got lost and got separated. One crash-landed, four are missing and haven't been heard from, and another one landed near a forest fire, mistaking it for the signal fire. Only one made it to Casas Grandes, and he just flew back to tell what happened."

"I'll be damned!" Whitlaw didn't have to feign surprise.

"See you later. Have to spread the word."

The little man should have been a reporter, Whitlaw thought, as he stepped inside the house. Glasheen was sitting on the edge of the bunk, examining the worn state of his shoes. "Should've brought m'work brogans from home," he said, thumbing back the loose edge of a sole.

Whitlaw related what he'd just heard.

"You don't mean it!" Glasheen looked shocked. "I'd be guessin' that's the first and last mission of the First Aero Squadron, then."

"I'd think a man of Foulois's experience would know better than to fly at night." Whitlaw dropped sideways onto a chair.

"Sometimes bosses get t'thinkin' they're as infallible as the Pope," Glasheen grunted. "But, gettin' back to more practical matters, you did say you wanted to go out to that spur tonight."

"Yes. There are two hand cars on a siding near here and we can borrow one of them before the moon is up. It'll take us a couple of hours to get there, taking turns pumping. We should make it to the spot before the midnight westbound from El Paso is scheduled to pass. We'll hide the hand car and spend the day taking a good, close look, then head back tomorrow night. We may not find anything, but we'll have satisfied ourselves there's nothing to be found."

By late afternoon, their preparations were complete. The gear was limited to what they could easily carry—two blankets, a short-handled shovel, pocket compass, a couple of sandwiches stuffed into the side pockets of their jackets, a bull's-eye lantern filled with coal oil, a small notebook and pencil, leather work gloves.

Whitlaw expected he'd have to do the gorilla's share of the pumping since Glasheen's wounded arm was not fully healed. "Might be a good idea to get a nap after supper, then we'll. . . ."

A sharp rap at the door interrupted him.

"It's open!"

A sergeant, wearing the insignia of the quartermaster corps, came in. "Colonel Slocum wants to see you," he said to Whitlaw.

"What now?"

"He didn't say, sir."

"You don't have to 'sir' me. I'm not in the Army."

"Force of habit, sir," the sergeant said, ducking out and leaving the door ajar.

"Why don't you slice some potatoes and open a can of beans," Whitlaw suggested. "I'll run over and see what he wants. Be right back."

"A few slices of bacon in the skillet would be tasty as

well," Glasheen said. "I'm becomin' a regular carnivore."

Colonel Slocum looked as if he'd had a long, hard day, and supper was nowhere in sight, Whitlaw thought, as he was ushered into the commandant's office. But, then, Slocum *always* looked that way.

"Whitlaw, I've got a favor to ask of you," the colonel said.

"Yes, sir."

"I want you to go into Mexico and rescue Maud Wright from those *Villistas*."

Before he could absorb this impact and begin to form questions, the colonel continued. "She went back south to her ranch with the expedition. The pilot who made it back says some of Villa's bunch have her ranch house surrounded. It's just her and her baby and a handful of Mexican hands that work for her, defending the place. They're under siege, but holding their own. Pershing's cavalry is a good day's ride from there. But that Jenny of yours, if it doesn't conk out, can be there in less than an hour."

"Colonel, I'll be glad to go," Whitlaw said, beginning to recover from the shock. "But do you expect me to lift the siege of an army by myself?"

"Hell, no!" He emphasized his words by smashing a fly on his desk with a rolled-up newspaper. "I'll give you the only Ben-A machine-gun that was left here. That should even the odds some. Take that Irishman with you. All I want you to do is keep those Mexicans at bay until a company of cavalry arrives. General Pershing has already started them." He shook his head and sat back in his swivel chair, its dry spring squeaking in protest. "I can't believe we've mounted an expedition to go after Villa and his boys, and we wind up having to rescue a civilian woman who probably shouldn't

be down there to begin with. But . . ."—he pursed his lips—
"she's one helluva woman. And who can blame a mother
for wanting to get back and see to the safety of her child?"

"Yes, sir." Although he admired the courage and tenacity
of the young widow as much as the commandant, Whitlaw
had serious misgivings about rushing into the midst of a
shooting war, or siege, as Slocum called it. Unless the bandits were simply harassing the widow and her men, Whitlaw
doubted he could do much about it, and he had no wish to
throw away his life, along with Glasheen's, in some heroic
gesture. He expressed these thoughts as carefully as he could.

"Dammit, Whitlaw, I wouldn't be calling on a civilian to
do a job that the Army should do, but you may have heard
by now that the First Aero Squadron is scattered all to hell
and gone. I have only one airplane here, and the pilot's so
exhausted, he's in no condition to fly."

"Don't you think this is foolhardy, a gallant effort that
will come to nothing, but will look good in the newspapers?" It was no way to address the commander, but
Whitlaw was old enough that he didn't have to take any
bovine defecation from anyone, military brass included. Besides, it was *his* life—not the colonel's—that would be on
the line.

Instead of blowing his top at the implication of a publicity
stunt, Colonel Slocum got up from his chair and tossed the
rolled newspaper down as he came around to the front of the
desk. "You and I are of the same generation," he said,
looking the still standing Whitlaw directly in the eyes. "Even
though we have very different backgrounds, I didn't have you
pegged as a coward. In fact, just the opposite. Anyone who
would take up flying at your age has to have a measure of
courage. And, need I remind you, that you have that Jenny
because of me? I could just as easily have confiscated it for

Army use, or given it to Lieutenant Scoggins's family."

"I appreciate that, sir." Whitlaw felt himself being whip-sawed by a combination of flattery and threat.

"One of my men will give you a quick course in the use of the machine-gun," the colonel was saying. "We'll, of course, supply anything else you may need . . . food, gasoline, oil, a mechanic to check your plane before you start . . . even leather jackets and helmets and sidearms, if you don't already have those things. I'll expect you to start right away, since time is of the essence." He was talking as if, by some unspoken signal, Whitlaw had consented to go. "It may be too late already, but we have to make the effort. I don't believe I'm mistaken when I say you and I still have a touch of gallantry, which may be lacking in modern warfare. I'd like to think that those of our age still live by a code of chivalry in spite of the brutality and inhumanity we see all around us."

"Yes, sir."

"I have a map. While not too detailed, it should suffice. The pilot, who got back here with this information, marked the spot where the Wright ranch is located. In a direct line, it's only fifty miles slightly southwest of here, right down the shallow valley."

Whitlaw looked at the map. It looked simple enough on paper. Most things of this nature did.

"You don't even have to land, if it looks too dangerous. Missus Wright could be dead, or taken away, or completely safe by the time you get there. Just assess the situation and do whatever you think best to scare them off until the mounted cavalry company arrives."

"And if I fail and don't come back, then you're not responsible since I'm a civilian volunteer," Whitlaw summarized dryly, rolling up the map.

"Exactly." The colonel gave him a tight smile that

stretched his grizzled mustache. He thrust out his hand. "Good luck!"

"We're postponing our little foray tonight. We have other business," Whitlaw said a few minutes later as he proceeded to relay the news to Glasheen.

"As you Yanks might say . . . you've got us into one helluva pickle," Glasheen commented.

"Then you'll go?" Whitlaw was relieved. "I can't force you. In fact, I'm not sure I even want to *urge* you. Risking my own life is one thing, but putting you in that kind of danger. . . ."

"The poor lass is a widow with a baby. I couldn't live with m'self if I didn't do what I could to help. If that were my wife, I'd like t'think one o' the boys back home would do the same for her."

Whitlaw's admiration for the Irishman took a giant leap upward. The man had never flown before yesterday, and now, at a word, was ready to fly into a hostile country on a life-and-death mission to help rescue a woman he'd seen only once. The spirit of medieval chivalry was alive and well.

Twenty minutes later, the Jenny was on the parade ground being gassed and oiled by two willing soldiers who'd helped push the plane from the adobe.

"Use the stepladder . . . don't put your foot on that wing!" Whitlaw cautioned one of the men. He turned back to the sergeant who was giving him some quick instructions on the use of the *Benet-Mercie* machine-gun.

"It's better operated by two men," the soldier was saying. "One to fire and one to load."

Whitlaw was paying close attention, trying to memorize the procedure. Where was he going to haul it? Weight was no problem since it barely topped twenty pounds. But should he stow it in the front cockpit with Glasheen? That

would give the Irishman something to think about beside
the fear of flying, and it would leave his own hands and feet
clear to fly the plane.

"Got it?" the sergeant asked.

Whitlaw nodded. "Leave it assembled and make sure it's
on safety. We'll tie it in the front cockpit." He hoisted the
gun and the metal box full of extra clips of ammunition. He
turned to Glasheen. "Just don't shoot the propeller off."

The propeller was pulled through twice before the engine fired. While the Jenny was warming up with the chocks
in place, Whitlaw lifted the gun into Glasheen's lap. With
the two supporting legs folded neatly alongside the barrel,
the gun was not much larger than an automatic rifle. The
metal box fit alongside the seat. Whitlaw was glad that the
cartridges, instead of being mounted on a limber belt that
could get tangled, were fastened thirty to a clip which were
fed into the side of the weapon, one clip at a time.

The Army outfitted both men with leather jackets, soft
leather helmets and gloves, along with a web belt, attached
canteen and leather holster containing the standard issue
.45 Colt automatic, with extra clips.

Before climbing into the rear cockpit, Whitlaw pulled
out his pistol and hefted it. He'd never fired an automatic.
It was a brutal-looking chunk of metal, and very heavy. He
wondered if he could hit anything with it. He hoped he
didn't have to find out. He shoved it back in place and secured the holster flap, then climbed into the seat, strapped
himself in, and checked the time—4:40 p.m. This would
have to be a quick trip to avoid darkness. He tucked the
hand-drawn map under his leg for quick reference, then
waved for the soldiers to yank the chocks. He slowly ad-
vanced the throttle. The OX-5 engine responded with a
full-throated roar and the Jenny began to roll.

Chapter Ten

The plane climbed to 5,000 feet before Whitlaw leveled off and headed south. While still on the ground, he had taken his compass and oriented it with the map, memorizing the heading that should take him to the ranch house. At cruising altitude, he once again held the vibrating compass and tried to align the nose of the plane on the heading. But it was a rough guess, at best. When he thought they were pointed in the right direction, he picked out a distant mountain peak to use for a guide. This plane needs a gimbaled compass, like a ship, he thought, if pilots want to fly by a plotted course.

The V-8 engine was running as smooth as he'd ever heard it. Although the sun was dropping down the western sky, from this altitude he seemed to have plenty of time before sunset. The sky was clear and yesterday's storm only a distant memory. Below, the valley floor was one large alluvial wash with no towns, sparse vegetation, and soil fading from a light chocolate to a dun color—a dry, barren plain.

Once more he began to climb, wanting to take the Jenny as high as possible to give himself the maximum view. Using his borrowed binoculars, he could probably spot the ranch house from several miles away. The prop blast got colder, and the rate of climb more sluggish. Could they top

8,000 feet, he wondered, watching the altimeter. He crouched in the cockpit, out of the wind, but still felt the cold through his cotton pants and on the exposed part of his face. Scoggins and others claimed the Jenny, at 90 horse power, was underpowered. Whitlaw wondered if it could clear even the foothills of the Sierra Madre. Now was his chance to find out, before they got to the large hills or mountains. He eased the wheel back and the Jenny reluctantly began to climb into the thin, cold air. Impatiently he pulled back harder on the column and the nose of the Jenny reared upward at a steeper angle, the engine roaring at full throttle. Whitlaw could see nothing on either side of him to judge their speed, but he sensed the craft slowing, like a car struggling up a steep hill. Suddenly they stopped. The plane hung motionless for a moment, and he realized they were in a stall. Then he felt them slipping backward. The nose fell over and the biplane began spiraling down in a headfirst spin toward the ground.

Panic shot through his stomach like a charge of electricity. He barely heard the wild yell from the front cockpit. The tan valley floor far below began to rotate in his vision. They were spinning out of control toward certain death. He gasped and fought the panic. There was still time. *Think! Think!* Scoggins had demonstrated once how to recover from a spin like this. *What did he do?* Whitlaw's memory was blank. He was so paralyzed with fear at the time, he hadn't noticed. But when they landed, Scoggins had insisted he memorize the procedure. What was it Scoggins had tried to drill into him over and over? The door to his memory was jammed.

If Glasheen would just stop that screaming! Whitlaw had no sensation of falling. It seemed they were flying straight ahead into a slowly rotating tan wall. The roar of the engine grew louder in his ears. Block it out! What had Scoggins repeated to him until he could say it in his sleep?

Suddenly the memory snapped back. He yanked the wheel to his chest. Full left rudder opposite from the spin. He slammed his foot on the rudder bar, and held his breath. The rotation slowed, and the ground fell away out of his line of sight as the nose came up. *Now . . . neutralize the wheel and reverse rudder.* The Jenny leveled out and flew smoothly. Whitlaw could feel the perspiration trickling down his forehead under the leather helmet. The voice of Scoggins came clearly to him now: "Don't bank more than thirty-five or forty degrees, since it takes three times as much aileron to get out of a bank than to get into it, and several seconds for them to work." And again: "When dropping your altitude in a spiral with a conservative amount of bank, hold it and correct for slip or skid with rudder or elevator. They are the only things that will work quick enough." He would remember that if he had to use a spiral to get down in a hurry.

Whitlaw ignored the gesticulations from the front seat and looked at his altimeter. It had unwound more than 2,000 feet. He was down to 5,500 feet. He took a deep breath. One more heart-stopping experience. But he would know what to do if it happened again. One other thing this had taught him: the Jenny was not capable of surmounting even the lower foothills of the Sierra. Foulois and his pilots, if they were to keep their planes in the air at all, would be confined to flying up and down this broad valley at relatively low altitudes.

The sun was gleaming off the barrel of the Ben-A poking up from the front cockpit, so that was still secure. Then he realized the sun was behind him. He had come out of the spin flying east, instead of south. With a light touch on the controls, he banked to the right until he had his low mountain landmark in sight again.

Back on course, he tried to think of something besides
his legs shaking from the effects of the scare. What would
he find when they arrived? Why was Villa picking on this
helpless woman? He had let her go once, to the United
States. Now she was back, and maybe he was irritated that a
mere woman would defy him and return to Mexico. Or,
maybe it was just his continuing campaign to kill all *gringos*
who came within his reach, such as mine supervisors and
others who were in Mexico, exploiting the wealth of his
country. Yet, the bandit leader had taken on more than he
could handle when he and his men attacked across the
border into Columbus.

Twenty minutes later, Whitlaw thought he spotted
something far ahead. He nosed the Jenny into a shallow
dive and descended another 2,000 feet. The plane droned
on. He pulled out his binoculars and focused them with one
hand. Through the whirling propeller, he could make out a
few tiny buildings. Stowing the glasses away, he checked his
watch. Even given the aerobatics he'd just performed, that
was about right. They should have covered a good 50 miles
by now. It was the only house in sight. That had to be it.
They were still a good distance off—too far to see if any
people or livestock were about. Even though he couldn't see
it, there had to be water on the property, judging from the
streaks of green and some trees. Maybe a spring or a small
stream running down from the mountains. Why would a
man and wife with a baby live in such a god-forsaken place?
Maybe they enjoyed solitude, maybe there was a good
market for whatever stock they raised. Maybe land was
cheap. If that were the case, they'd certainly paid a high
price for it now. But that wasn't his concern. Maud
Wright's husband was dead. She and her child, if they were

still alive, were at the mercy of a bunch of no-conscience bloody rebels who would think no more of killing them than of stepping on a scorpion.

He stared at the tiny buildings, growing larger by the minute, again wondering what he was doing here. At age sixty-four he should have been sitting in a porch swing with his grandkids on his knee, smoking his pipe, and regaling them with tales of his adventures on the trains. Or drinking beer and playing cards with his old cronies. He had no business piloting this aircraft. This was the future. He was a child of the 19th Century, an orphan in the 20th.

As they drew nearer, he let the Jenny slide to 1,500 feet, and details became clearer. The ranch house was a one-story adobe affair with a flat roof, wooden porch, and adobe corral, with scattered small wooden outbuildings. A tiny stream had created a pond surrounded by trees and some grass. That could explain why this ranch was a favorite stop of the roaming rebels—it was apparently the only source of water for miles. And they surely hated the *gringos* who controlled it. The whole revolution, even among the warring factions, was based on the concept that all land in Mexico belonged to the Mexicans who lived on it and worked it— not to the *patróns,* not to the wealthy families, not to the mine owners, and especially not to the Americans who came and took what they wanted and treated the people like slaves. A more equitable distribution of land was what it was all about. The orgy of blood-letting that had been going on for several years was frustration turned loose, something akin to the reign of terror that had followed the French Revolution a century and a quarter before.

This fleeting thought escaped him as the ranch grew closer. At first it appeared deserted, but then he noticed the tiny figures of horses moving about in the corral. He dropped to within 500 feet and leaned into a wide, left bank. Men were squatting around two campfires, cooking an evening meal, protected from the ranch house by the trees and an adobe wall. Whitlaw had a glimpse of startled faces looking up as he turned away and flew a mile south. Banking around, he steadied the plane and held the wheel with his knees as he took the binoculars in both hands and tried to focus on the men. With the vibrations and the bouncing, he found it very difficult to see anything clearly. He suspected he and Glasheen had arrived while the house was still under siege, but he had to be sure those men at the cook fires were not just ranch hands. He set the binoculars in his lap and guided the plane in for another pass. Holding the binoculars with one hand, he caught a jiggled picture of red saddle blankets thrown about with the saddles under a tree. Maud had told them this was the mark of Villa's men. Any lingering doubts were erased when he saw the puffs of smoke from several rifles as the plane roared overhead. He held his breath until they were out of range. If a bullet hit the fuel tank, it was all over. Then he noticed three jagged rips in the fabric of the lower left wing.

"Damn!"

He flew east for at least three miles, hoping the Mexicans would think he'd been scared off. They probably assumed he was one of the hated *gringos,* since Americans were the only ones who had aircraft. But, unlike the military aircraft, his Jenny contained no numbers or markings of any kind and was painted a light sand color.

If Maud Wright and her defenders were already dead or captured, those *Villistas* would not be camped there. It was time to take action. He would chance one or two more passes, this time with Glasheen using the Ben-A machine-gun. Glasheen glanced back and Whitlaw motioned for him to get the weapon ready. The Irishman nodded and began working on the gun.

Whitlaw gave him a couple of minutes to insert a clip and flip the safety off. By hand signals, he indicated for Glasheen to fire over the left side of the plane, easier for a right-handed shooter. Glasheen unfastened his seat belt and raised himself to a kneeling position that would give him a better angle of fire over the lip of the cowling. He took the precaution of re-arranging the rope that secured the gun. Neither of them had ever fired this weapon before, but since the gun was so light, it was reputed to have a fearsome recoil.

When Glasheen signaled he was ready, Whitlaw made a long, sweeping bank toward the house, several miles to the west. The sun would not be a factor, since it had already dropped behind the western mountain range. Whitlaw dared not throttle back too much. The men on the ground had a stable firing position and would have no trouble hitting their low-flying target. If the Jenny were brought down by gunfire, he and Glasheen, if they survived, would not stand a chance against the armed bandits.

His heart was pounding as he carefully came around and swept down toward the ranch house. He had to hold his angle of bank just enough for Glasheen to fire downward, but not so steep that his unstrapped gunner would lose his balance. Left wings tilted down, he roared low over the men below. The machine-gun began its chatter, and Whitlaw saw spurts of dust and chips of adobe flying as the *Villistas* scrambled for cover.

Whitlaw pulled the plane up and away. A thirty-round burst from one clip didn't take long. Glasheen was nodding and grinning as he thrust the end of a second clip into the side of the Ben-A and swung the thick stock to his shoulder, ready for another pass.

A volley of gunfire greeted their second run. Whitlaw felt a lead slug strike the bottom of his iron seat, numbing a spot on his butt for several seconds. By then they were past and he looked back. One man was sprawled near the dusty corral, and another was limping away, dragging one leg. Glasheen's massive torso had absorbed the recoil and kept the gun as much on target as possible, considering they were traveling nearly 70 miles an hour. Even so, Whitlaw thought the hits were probably due as much to luck as anything else. He flew north for about five miles, glanced toward the red glow of the departed sun, then pulled out his watch. They'd been in the air nearly an hour and twenty minutes. The effective flight time of this plane was only two and a half hours. He had slightly less than one hour left. He'd experienced running out of gas once this week and didn't want to repeat that, especially in Mexico. He should start back for the border right now. But he couldn't resist having one more go at the *Villistas*. He held up a finger to signal Glasheen that they would strafe the bandits one more time.

The *Villistas* had been surprised before, but now they had their arsenal prepared. Whitlaw swooped low over them, the Ben-A bucking against the stocky Irishman's shoulder and empty shell casings spewing out as the machine-gun did its deadly work. The bandits fired continuously as the Jenny passed over. Although Whitlaw felt nothing, he knew they had to have taken some hits. Riflemen could hardly miss at that range.

Time to make for home, he thought, climbing away from the ranch house. But he was headed south already, so he swung west for a minute to see if he could spot the approach of Pershing's cavalry that Slocum had assured him was on the way.

From a height of 2,500 feet, he could see several miles

west and south, but saw only the empty, arid valley with scrub and small timber on the slopes of the purpling foothills. No telltale dust to reveal approaching horsemen, no ant-size figures crawling across the waste. Slocum had estimated the cavalry was at least a day's ride away, but that was third-hand information and probably just a guess on someone's part.

He could waste no more time looking. They had to head for the border. The sun had disappeared behind the Sierras some time ago and twilight was fast cloaking them in shadows. It would be full dark before they arrived back in Columbus, but he was confident he could find it by the lights. The plane had no lights and he couldn't read the altimeter. Landing would be a challenge, but that couldn't be helped. One or two planets were already visible in the clear sky. If he got confused, he could always navigate by following the north star. While he still had a little light, he held up the map and took a close look. The little village of Ascension looked to be only a few miles south and east of here. But, with the fading daylight, and the tendency of adobe buildings to blend into the landscape from this height, he could see nothing in that direction.

In the gathering darkness, he saw a six-inch, yellowish-blue flame shooting from the exhaust pipes on either side of the engine. Flying in the dark would not be a problem, but landing would. And what of Maud Wright and her loyal Mexicans? He had not even seen them, but had given their attackers something to think about. Would the cavalry column arrive in time?

He sniffed. Something burning. Oil. The engine was overheating! Before he could react to cut power and keep the engine from being ruined, it coughed twice and the propeller whipped to a stop.

"Oh, *shit!*" And he meant that sincerely.

He quickly looked for a place to land. They were still 3,000 feet up, and the light Jenny would glide a good ways, but he didn't want to come down in the vicinity of the ranch house if he could help it. He knew he was close enough that the Mexicans on the ground had heard the droning engine abruptly stop. In the eerie silence, the only sound was a silky whistling of the wind through the wire struts as the Jenny began sinking gradually toward the darkening earth and the *Villistas*.

Chapter Eleven

Whitlaw's mind was racing. He thought he was still south of the ranch house. He'd flown southwest for at least five or six minutes, maybe six or seven miles, to see if he could spot the cavalry column. Then he'd banked a turn of 160 degrees and started home. How long had he been on this northerly course? Two minutes, maybe? No more than three, he estimated, although he hadn't really been paying attention. Should he change course to make sure he didn't come down near the ranch house?

The gliding Jenny seemed to be losing airspeed. *Keep the nose down a little. . . .* He tried a tentative bank to the left, but the controls were mushy. *Careful, don't let it stall and fall into a spin. . . .* He carried a few stick matches for his pipe, and thought of trying to strike one to read the altimeter. But the rushing wind smothered that idea. The moon wasn't up yet. Looking over the right side, he could barely make out some lighter streaks of bare, sandy soil. To the left were darker patches, apparently vegetation where the foothills flattened into the valley. He would try to aim for the lighter streaks. He pushed the wheel forward to increase their speed and rate of descent. Had it been light and had he had power, he might have tried to side-slip down. But with a dead stick in the dark, his best chance was to glide straight in. If only Scoggins were in the front seat to take over the controls! The keening wind increased to a higher pitch.

"James, m'lad," a strained voice came from the front cockpit in the unnatural quiet. "I can't say it's been a pleasure knowin' ya, but this sure beats bein' cut down by a British Enfield. Mighty spectacular ending, I'd say. I just hope somebody relays the sad news to me darlin' Annie."

"Cut out that kind of talk! We're not going to die." Whitlaw wished he felt the assurance that was in his voice. "I'm going to set this thing down as lightly as a falling leaf." Might as well make it sound really good.

Several seconds of silence followed, then Whitlaw thought of something. "Better hang that machine-gun over the side with a rope. Don't want it banging into you when we land."

Glasheen dutifully slipped the Ben-A outside the cockpit.

As the Jenny sank into the darkness, Whitlaw glanced over one side and then the other, trying to pick out a likely spot, desperately hoping his depth perception would kick in when they were close enough to spot the trees. He needed a few seconds to flare out and stall, then drop the last several feet. "Protect your face. Make sure your lap belt is tight!" he called forward. "We'll be touching down in a minute or two!"

"I should've listened to m'mother and become a priest," came the groaning voice from forward.

Whitlaw held his breath, both hands clenching the wheel. Large mesquite trees suddenly rushed past beneath them. "Not yet . . . not yet," he breathed, his eyes glued on the pale streak of light, sandy soil ahead. "Now!" He pulled back. The nose came up and the plane nearly stalled as it flared out. His stomach lurched as they suddenly dropped ten feet. They hit with a crash, bounced, and came down again, the landing gear collapsing. He was slung forward, banging his head on the metal rim of the instrument panel as the Jenny plowed through the desert scrub on her belly, tearing off the lower left wing.

He was barely conscious when the plane jolted to a halt. Several seconds later, his reeling senses began to recover. He sat up and felt his forehead. Wet, warm blood was trickling from a cut, but his leather helmet had taken most of the blow. His arms and legs seemed to be intact and he was breathing. "Glasheen! You all right?" he cried, pulling off the goggles that were askew on his face.

No answer.

"Glasheen!" His head hurt like hell and a knot was rising just above the hairline. His hands were shaking as he fumbled to unbuckle his seat belt. Fears mounting for his friend, Whitlaw climbed out of the canted fuselage and tripped over the machine-gun dangling in the way.

"Glasheen!" Whitlaw reached into the front, grabbed the slumped figure by the shoulders.

"*Aahhh!*"

Whitlaw's heart jumped. "You hurt bad?"

After several seconds' hesitation, Glasheen's husky voice responded just above a whisper. "I'm either in purgatory or hell, 'cause I'm hurtin' like the very divil."

"Where are you hurt?"

"M'head and m'knees are painin' me for m'sins."

"You may be suffering for your sins, but you're not in hell or purgatory yet," Whitlaw said, relieved that the Irishman was alive and evidently not mortally injured. "You break a leg?"

"Can't rightly tell," he replied, loosening his seat belt and attempting to stand. "Oh!" he cringed from sudden pain. "Might've cracked m'kneecaps. Front panel got shoved back on me." He put an arm around Whitlaw's shoulders and was half dragged out of the cockpit. His heavy foot promptly went through the fabric of the lower wing, and he staggered against the fuselage. "Set 'er down as light as a fallin' leaf, ya say? I'm thankin' m'guardian angel y'didn't make a *hard* landing."

Whitlaw took the bulk of the Irishman's weight on himself and they tottered from the plane. He let Glasheen down on the sandy earth about twenty yards away. "Be right back." Removing the leather helmet, he mopped his bloody face with a bandanna, then put the helmet back on and hurried to the Jenny. The strong odor of gasoline smote his nose. Ruptured tank or fuel line. He reached into the rear cockpit and flipped off the switch. Maybe the rushing air had cooled the engine enough to prevent it catching fire.

He slung both canvas-covered canteens over his shoulder, then pulled out his jackknife and cut the twisted rope that held the machine-gun. His injured head throbbing from exertion, he carried the Ben-A and the canteens and set them beside the dazed Glasheen. He went back for the box of clips, praying that the plane would not explode in a ball of fire. Even if he were able to get clear, it would be a bright signal in the night sky for nearby *Villistas*.

Whitlaw plopped down, panting, beside Glasheen. His night vision improved as full darkness settled, the clear sky aglitter with stars. With the disappearance of the sun, the mild warmth of the March day passed into the chill of the high desert night. He dared not build a fire until he figured out where they were. "Can you walk?"

"Give me a hand up."

The Irishman was much shorter, but he had to weigh all of 200 pounds. Glasheen gained his feet, leaning heavily on

Whitlaw. He took a few halting steps. "By the saints, it's pure agony. But I can go a bit, provided we don't have to walk to Columbus."

That's just what we'll have to do, Whitlaw thought, but said: "We'll move west a ways, into the foothills. Might find better cover and water." He looked for the north star to get his bearings, found it, then guided Glasheen west, weaving slowly among the low desert scrub. His leather jacket felt good in the chill. In two or three more months, this desert would be baking.

In a quarter hour, Whitlaw began to breathe a little easier. Perhaps they'd crash-landed far enough from the Wright house that the soldiers hadn't heard or seen them descend. After all, during the last few minutes they had glided noiselessly.

At a shuffle, carrying the Ben-A by the barrel and dragging the ammo box by one handle, they managed to move about 400 yards. Desert scrub gave way to a scattering of small trees as the terrain tilted slightly upward.

"This is as good a place as any to stop and rest," Whitlaw panted. "We'll move on when the moon comes up and we can see." He set down the 27 pound machine-gun and unbuttoned his leather jacket. The ear flaps of his helmet were turned up so he could hear. He checked his 1911 Model Colt .45 to be sure it contained a loaded clip.

A short time later, when the perspiration was drying on Whitlaw's body and he was beginning to stiffen up, a pale light appeared in the sky. The gibbous moon gradually rose, paling the starry firmament and casting a silvery hue over creosote bush and sage. It gave them a ghostly view of the sloping valley to the east. He had no idea which way the ranch house lay, but guessed it was still north and a little east of their position.

The talkative Glasheen was strangely quiet. Whitlaw wondered if he might have suffered a slight concussion. "How are you feeling now?"

"The grenadiers are beating bass drums in m'head," he answered. "And the wee folk are usin' m'kneecaps for hurling practice." He sighed. "But it's thankful I am for all o' that. Just to be alive on God's green earth is enough."

Whitlaw smiled in the darkness. He wished he'd known this man twenty-five years before. There were many Irishmen on the UP, but none quite like him.

"I do believe you've scuffed your flyin' machine beyond repair," Glasheen added.

"I'll have to inspect it in daylight." Whitlaw realized with a pang that Glasheen was probably right. Perhaps his piloting days were over.

He reached up and touched his head. The cut had stopped bleeding since he'd been pressing the bandanna to it, but his face felt sticky with crusty blood. He wanted to wash it off, but knew they might need every drop of canteen water before this was over. He wondered about their next move. While darkness covered their movements, they should go as far as possible into the foothills to avoid Mexican bandits. His adrenaline was ebbing; he was sagging with fatigue. He dared not get too comfortable, or he'd fall asleep. Glasheen may have suffered a slight concussion. It was going to be a long night. He was definitely getting too old for all this.

Suddenly his heart rate jumped and adrenaline began to flow. Voices! He was no longer sleepy.

"Do y'think . . . ?" Glasheen began.

"Sshhh!" Whitlaw put a hand up for silence. "Listen!"

Nothing. He strained to catch any sound, turning his head this way and that. Then it came again—faint voices, speaking Spanish. For several seconds, the colder, heavier, mountain air, sliding downslope, carried the sounds away from them. Then a horse snorted, not fifty yards distant, and Whitlaw froze.

Dim figures of a half dozen riders appeared out of a desert wash, moving toward them at a walk. Now the voices came clearly on the night air. Although Whitlaw didn't understand much Spanish, he caught a word or two of the conversation and realized they were searching for the downed plane.

Whitlaw looked around desperately for a place to hide. But any movement now would be plainly visible in the moonlight.

Chapter Twelve

The riders were coming directly toward them. The two men couldn't hug the ground in the chaparral and avoid being stepped on. Whitlaw had a second or two of indecision. If they moved slowly and kept low, perhaps they could edge out of the way without being seen by the Mexicans who were distracted by conversation.

Whitlaw tapped Glasheen and motioned for him to go upslope. But he'd forgotten the Irishman couldn't crawl on bad knees; he could barely walk. And they dared not leave the machine-gun behind.

"Slow," Whitlaw whispered, pushing Glasheen who struggled to his feet. Whitlaw hooked the canteens over Glasheen's head, then grabbed the ammo box by one handle and the Ben-A in the other hand. The moonlight was deceptive. Black shadows ten yards away sharply etched the outline of a desert wash. Maybe it was deep enough to hide them. The horsemen would have to ride around. Two crouching steps . . . five steps, dragging the gun by the barrel. He was forced to stop and wait for Glasheen. Whitlaw heard the *jingle* of a bit chain, the *squeak* of leather. The low, casual voices suddenly stopped. *"¡Alto!"* came the sharp command.

"Go!" Whitlaw snapped. "To the ditch!"

Excited shouting behind them. Glasheen tripped and

tumbled headfirst out of sight into the arroyo. A shot cracked. Whitlaw dove for the lip of the wash and slid in with the gun and ammo box banging his ribs.

Thudding hoofs. No time to set up the Ben-A. Before Whitlaw could even get right side up, a .45 blasted twice next to him. Glasheen was firing at the horsemen. Whitlaw threw himself against the sloping, chest-high dirt bank. The automatic bucked in his hand as he fired in the general direction of movement. The rush was checked, and, with wild yells and a few answering shots, the horsemen wheeled and scattered. Whitlaw fired twice more, then slid several feet to the right so the attackers couldn't zero in on the muzzle flashes. His breath was coming in gasps. The horsemen had to be *Villistas*. But, even if they weren't, they'd fired first. He heard yelling back and forth and crashing in the brush and thudding hoof beats. The surprised Mexicans were moving out of range.

"Damn!" Whitlaw's heart was pounding. He slipped below the lip of the dry wash. "Keep your head down," he cautioned.

"The bla'guards are on the run!"

"I doubt it. They're just regrouping," Whitlaw panted, feeling in his pocket for another clip. "They know there can be only two of us, if we were in that plane. And we fired on them with a machine-gun. They'll have their revenge now that we're on the ground, outnumbered."

"B'God, let 'em come!" Glasheen said. "M'knees and head are feelin' better already!"

Whitlaw said nothing, remembering how the *Villistas* had charged up the streets of Columbus into the teeth of several machine-guns. Crazed with hate, blind for booty, or just wild and reckless, they were a formidable enemy who had no fear for their lives. "Keep watch while I set up the Ben-A,"

Whitlaw said. "This might equalize the odds a little. When they get organized, they could try to overrun us since there's plenty of moonlight now." He checked the gun to be sure no dirt was in it, propped the two folding legs up to steady the end of the barrel, and lifted it over the lip of the arroyo. He set the ammo box by his feet, extracted one of several remaining clips, and carefully inserted it into the slot in the right side of the receiver.

The Mexicans had retreated beyond earshot. If they made an attack, he hoped it would come from the same direction. But he would surely hear them in time to shift the gun if he had to. *What the hell am I doing here? I'm no soldier. This whole thing is too bizarre to be believed.*

In spite of what Glasheen seemed to think, it was a vain hope that the *Villistas* had been run off for keeps. Their business was murder and plunder. If their so-called Army of the North ever succeeded in bringing down the *de facto* Carranza government in Mexico City, it would make little difference to these illiterate bandits. If a stable government were somehow achieved, their lucrative careers would be threatened or ended. They thrived on turmoil and revolution. Force was the only thing they understood. At the moment, two model 1911 Colt .45 automatics and a French-designed machine-gun were all that stood between two older *gringos* and these ruthless bandits. Whitlaw would rather have faced wild boars or mountain lions. At least they would be somewhat predictable. He'd discovered there was no outguessing a Mexican or an Indian. Their reasoning and thought processes were completely different. They operated on some pattern unknown to him. Instead of seeking revenge for the air attack, it wouldn't be unlike them to shrug and go back to their campfires and blankets for the night, and continue their leisurely siege of the ranch house. He doubted Villa himself was with them, or they wouldn't be following the path of least resistance.

He slid to a sitting position beneath the stock of the Ben-A.

"Will the bla'guards make another rush at us?" Glasheen asked, hefting the Colt.

"I don't know. They could overwhelm us in one concerted rush. But as long as our scorpion can sting, they might decide they don't really want us that bad."

"We've not a place to go," Glasheen said. "They could wait us out. If they found the airplane, they know the machine-gun is gone."

"Yeah. My guess is they've left several men at the ranch house to keep Maud Wright and her crew pinned down and sent the rest to find us."

"*Sshhh!* Listen!" Glasheen held up a hand.

They held their collective breath. Dead silence except for the scurrying of some nocturnal desert creature. Even the wind was still.

"M'imagination playin' me false again," Glasheen said, slumping back against the dirt bank, holding the Colt in his lap.

Several minutes dragged by and Whitlaw began to sag. The longer they went without an attack, the more fatigued he felt. His adrenaline had ebbed, and he was feeling all the aches and bruises received in the crash landing. The night air slid down the mountainside and filled their dry arroyo, chilling the sweat on his body. Whitlaw reached into a pocket of his leather jacket for the gloves he'd pulled off just after the wreck. His hand encountered a paper-wrapped lump. Sandwiches! He'd forgotten all about them. "How about some supper?" He held up a sandwich.

"B'God, I think I will." Glasheen reached for it, unwrapped the waxed paper, and took a huge bite. "Ah, bacon and peanut butter and mustard . . . m'favorite."

"Are they both the same?"

"You betcha . . . as you Yanks say."

"I think I'll make the sandwiches next time." But hunger made even this combination appetizing he quickly discovered. He began to eat, wondering if there would be a next time. For all he knew, the *Villistas* were carefully surrounding them.

"What'll we be doin' now?" Glasheen mumbled around a mouthful of food.

Whitlaw had been pondering the same question. "If they don't come back before moonset, we'll take the Ben-A and move south and west, staying in cover as best we can. That direction should be our best chance of meeting up with some of our own troops."

Glasheen took a sip from his canteen. "What might be our chances of getting out of here alive?" he asked.

"Very good," Whitlaw answered, trying to remain upbeat for Glasheen's sake. A defeatist attitude would not help either of them.

"Have you ever wondered what dyin' will be like?"

"Sure. Often. Especially as I get older."

"Do y'recall the Gospel stories of Jesus raisin' the dead?"

"Yes."

"I know He did that to show He was God, but it appears t'me He didn't do those people any favors."

"How so?"

"B'God, Lazarus was a friend o' His."

"Yeah."

"The poor lad had suffered and died once. Then Jesus finally gets there, three days later, and brings him back to life, so he can live a few years longer and die again. That seems a bit harsh, just so Jesus could prove His power over death."

Whitlaw chuckled. "Never thought of it that way."

"And d'ye suppose Lazarus remembered where his soul had gone those three days his body was a-rottin' in the tomb? You suppose, if he'd gone to heaven, he came back a-braggin' about that fact to his friends?"

"I'd have to speculate he didn't recollect that adventure. The Gospel writer doesn't say."

"Strange, the things that go through a man's mind when he's likely to be facin' his own demise," Glasheen said, his low voice husky.

"I don't think you and I will have to worry about dying twice," Whitlaw said. "Unless we let this prey on our minds. As the bard says . . . 'The coward dies many times before his death. The valiant never taste of death but once.' Besides, you were saying good bye in the airplane. And here I've gotten you through this far, only scuffed around the edges."

Glasheen laughed quietly. "That y'have, lad, that y'have." Then he sighed, carefully wrapped up the remainder of his sandwich, and shoved it into his pocket. "I hope m'guardian angel hasn't deserted me as well as m'appetite."

"Since we volunteered to come and rescue Maud Wright, do you think we should still try?" Whitlaw asked. "We may be outnumbered, but we have the machine-gun, and the element of surprise."

"And they have horses and many rifles. That Ben-A jams easily. If it does, it would be like stubbing our toe in front of a speeding train. Besides, we don't even know which direction the ranch house is from here."

The gleam of moonlight on a rifle barrel gave Whitlaw just enough warning. He threw himself against Glasheen. Even as they were falling, the quiet night erupted in a roar of white light and thunderous explosions.

Chapter Thirteen

Bullets slammed into the bank, showering dirt on the two men.

Reacting with the speed of desperation, Whitlaw rolled over and pulled his Colt. Without looking, he reached up over the lip of the wash and emptied his clip in the general direction of the attack. From the glint off a gun barrel, he knew the *Villistas* had crept to within twenty yards. His spray of bullets was answered by a yell of pain and some cursing in Spanish.

Glasheen was suddenly at his side.

"Keep your head down!" Whitlaw warned, his voice drowned by a fusillade that tore at the earth, kicking up sand and bits of mesquite. Whitlaw slid to the bottom of the wash. "When I give the word, start firing. I want to make a grab for the Ben-A."

There was a sudden lull in the firing. Whitlaw's ears were ringing. "Get ready. . . . Now!"

Glasheen's Colt banged away. Whitlaw leapt up the other side of the wash and lunged for the machine-gun. A bullet knocked the stock away from his hand, but he managed to grab the receiver and yank the gun down on top of him. "Got it!" He kept the mechanism from contacting the dirt. Glasheen fired twice more, then the Colt's slide jumped back and locked open after the last round. He reached for another clip on his belt.

Whitlaw was fumbling with the Ben-A. If the attackers decided to rush their position, two Colts would not hold them off. "Here, you take this," Whitlaw said, shoving the machine-gun up to Glasheen. "It's ready. Give me your pistol." They made the quick exchange. The Irishman had some experience firing the fully automatic weapon, and was strong enough to hold it on target.

Just as Glasheen muscled the gun into position on the lip of the wash, the *Villistas* came charging and yelling. The *Benet-Mercie* began to stutter its message of death. Whitlaw was blasting away with a Colt in each hand. Several dark figures pitched over in the brush. A slug kicked dirt into Whitlaw's mouth. Another bullet nicked the top of his ear. It felt like a bee sting. But the attack faltered within ten yards and broke, the remaining uninjured *Villistas* dodging sideways into cover of the mesquite and the irregular ground. A second 30-shot clip was quickly used up and the machine-gun fell silent, then they heard crashing and thudding in the brush and several high-pitched yells as the remaining *Villistas* struggled back out of the way. Whitlaw felt unco-ordinated, trying to release the clip from the butt of a Colt and pull another off his belt, when he realized the attackers had stopped firing and those who were able were fleeing. He could barely see their shadowy figures moving away in the moonlight.

Glasheen inserted another clip into the Ben-A.

"Hold your fire. We might need that ammo later," Whitlaw said. "They're gone for now." He took a deep breath and tried to steady his pounding heart. "Guess they were surprised at our firepower." He became suddenly aware of the sting on his left ear and put a hand up to feel the warm blood. "Damn! I'm a bloody mess." He yanked out his dirty bandanna and pressed it to the wound.

Without waiting for moonset, the two men clambered out of the arroyo. Banking on the assumption that the *Villistas* had fled, Whitlaw and Glasheen took their canteens, pistols, and the Ben-A, and headed southwest. In the moonlit darkness, Whitlaw was unsure of directions, but finally brushed against a knee-high barrel cactus—the so-called "compass cactus" that tends to lean toward the south as it grows. Then he was sure of his route. He could only guess how far they traveled in the next two hours, since Glasheen's painful knees forced him to walk slowly. Although the terrain was not unusually rough, they stumbled often in the dark.

"*Ahhh!* I've got to stop and rest," Glasheen groaned, slipping off the straps of the two canteens.

"Your knees hurting?"

"Not so bad. I just feel like I'm carrying a hod o' bricks on m'shoulders."

Whitlaw slipped out a match, struck it, and looked at his watch—12:40 a.m. "We'll find some shelter where we can sleep a while, out of sight." He scouted until he came across a thick stand of mesquite, and they crawled under. As a precaution, he set up the Ben-A and shoved in a full clip, engaging the safety. "This'll be handy, just in case . . . ," he mumbled. He was glad Glasheen had proposed they stop. His own legs felt rubbery. He thought the frigid air had helped slow the bleeding where the bullet had nicked the top of his ear.

"Bloody and battered, but still unbowed." Whitlaw laughed as he squirmed into a somewhat comfortable position. "Sleep well."

There came only a muffled grunt from a few feet away. In less than two minutes, he heard the steady breathing of sleep.

Whitlaw ate the rest of his sandwich, wondering if they had traveled at least two or three miles in the two hours since the fight. As fatigued as he was, sleep didn't come immediately. He had an unusual fear of poisonous snakes, but took comfort in the thought that it might be too cold for any rattlers to be abroad this night.

The next thing Whitlaw knew, it was full daylight. He rolled over with a groan, hurting in at least twenty places. He pulled out his Elgin and wound it from long habit. It was 6:18. Glasheen still slept. They had to be on the move. He cringed at the Irishman's evident pain as he gently shook him awake.

"I'm stiffer than me mother-in-law's corset!" he gasped.

Whitlaw helped knead the big muscles in his arms and legs until Glasheen loosened up enough to roll out from under the mesquite thicket. Then they helped each other stand. They were tottering like two ninety-year-olds. Glasheen took a swig of water from a canteen and rubbed a few drops on his eyelids.

"I should have remembered the binoculars," Whitlaw said, looking around. "Left 'em in the plane."

"Can't think of everything."

They walked for a few minutes and gradually their aching bodies limbered up. Their breath steamed in the frosty air, and Whitlaw was again thankful they were wearing the leather flying jackets.

"Look!" Glasheen stopped dead. They had stumbled onto a dirt road. But he wasn't pointing at the road. Coming toward them was a Mexican leading a burro hitched to a two-wheeled wooden cart.

Whitlaw yanked his Colt. "*¡Alto!*"

The peasant stopped, looking fearfully at the drawn

159

Colt. The mustachioed man wore cotton clothing, a large-brimmed hat, and leather sandals. He didn't appear to be armed.

Whitlaw struggled with his nearly non-existent Spanish. *"Americanos,"* he said, pointing to himself and Glasheen. *"Otro americanos. ¿Donde?"*

The Mexican continued to stare at the gun as if he expected to be shot any second.

Whitlaw groped under his jacket to his pants pocket and came out with five silver dollars—all he had. He held out the coins. "Take us to the American soldiers and these are yours." From the looks of this man, five dollars was a sizeable bribe.

The peasant continued to stare without moving or speaking.

"We're a bloody sight for a man t'come upon this early in the mornin'," Glasheen said in a low voice. Whitlaw had forgotten what he must look like with dried blood all over his face and coat from the scalp and ear wounds.

Whitlaw again shoved the silver toward him.

"Sí," the man finally said, coming cautiously closer and reaching for the money.

Whitlaw tossed three silver dollars at the *peón's* feet. "You get the other two when we reach the soldiers," Whitlaw said, closing his fist over the remaining coins. He still held the pistol. "The American soldiers . . . *comprende?"*

"Sí. I speak English, *señor. Un poco."*

"Bueno. This man is hurt and must ride in your cart."

The Mexican motioned for Glasheen to get in. Whitlaw piled the Ben-A and the canteen in with him. They started off in the direction the Mexican had been going, Whitlaw walking to one side and still holding the Colt.

As they plodded along, the peasant continued to glance

to left and right and at the slopes to their left. He even looked behind him several times.

"What's the matter?"

"Nada, señor."

"What are you looking for?"

"The *Villistas* will shoot me if they catch me helping *americanos*," he said. Then he shrugged. "But you pay much money."

The sun rose and warmed the travelers so that Whitlaw had to unbutton his jacket. By midday he wished for more food, but waved off the offer to share Glasheen's remaining half sandwich.

Whitlaw's sense of direction was askew; he got the feeling they were headed back in the same general direction they had just traversed. Was this man leading them into a trap? Whitlaw was becoming increasingly uneasy, when the sudden sound of galloping horses reached his ears, and four soldiers rode into view from the scrub ahead. Relief flooded over him when he recognized the olive drab and the peaked straight brim hats of the American cavalry.

The riders reined up in a swirl of dust. "Ho! What's this?"

"B'God, it's glad t'see ya, we are!" Glasheen exclaimed, trying to heave himself out of the cart.

"Who're you men?"

"Flyers from Columbus. Crashed our Jenny last night."

The sergeant in charge of the patrol urged his mount closer and peered at the face of Whitlaw. "By thunder, man, you look like you lost a fight with a mountain lion. So that was you who strafed those *Villistas* at the ranch house!"

"Yeah. What about Maud Wright? Is she alive?"

"Alive and safe, thanks to you two . . . both her and her baby," a corporal said, grinning. "You put the fear of God

161

and machine-guns into those greasers. And we run off the rest of 'em."

"We found your plane not a quarter mile from the house," the sergeant continued. "Looked like a damned sieve! But what did the real damage was the three bullets through your radiator."

"Figured it was something like that," Whitlaw said.

"We found three dead *Villistas* laid out near the corral, and . . . ," the corporal began.

"You want to tell us about the six other bodies we found a few hundred yards out in the brush?" the sergeant interrupted. "And what two old civilians are doing here to begin with?"

Whitlaw briefly related the story of their mission and adventure of the previous night.

"That Ben-A saved your hides," the sergeant said. "Come on. We'll take you with us. You look a little the worse for wear."

"What about the *Villistas?*"

"Well, this batch of them is either dead or long gone," the sergeant said, taking the machine-gun and handing it up to a soldier.

Whitlaw gratefully accepted a hand up to ride double behind the corporal. It took two men to get Glasheen into the saddle, and a private vaulted up behind him.

"The ranch is only a short ways. We captured a few extra horses so you two can ride with us back to Babicora in the morning."

"Where?"

"San Miguel de Babicora. It's in the mountains west of here. William Randolph Hearst has a house there. Rumor has it Villa was seen in that area."

One of the soldiers hoisted the ammo box across his pommel.

"Move out!"

Whitlaw turned and flipped the two remaining silver dollars to the *peón* who caught them deftly. "You're as good as your word, old man."

But, with no acknowledgment, the Mexican was already leading his burro away down the road.

Chapter Fourteen

The mogul locomotive labored up one of the switchbacks to the Cumbre Pass in the Sierra Madre Mountains. It trailed a mixed train of eight livestock cars, four boxcars, and a caboose. The stock cars were filled to capacity with cavalry horses, the boxcars piled with gear. Soldiers and several civilians rode in whatever remaining space they could find. The black troopers of the 10th Cavalry had chosen to spread out on the roofs of the stock cars that carried their mounts. Here they talked and laughed, shared tobacco, and generally relaxed out of sight of the officers, some of whom occupied the boxcar just ahead of the caboose. The wind was still, but the train's speed of less than ten miles an hour stirred a chill breeze that caused a few of the soldiers to sit on their hands or thrust them into their pockets.

In the boxcar behind the string of eight stock cars rode Whitlaw, Glasheen, Maud Wright and her baby, three of her Mexican hands, a dozen troopers, and three officers.

"Lieutenant, why didn't you just drop us off at Dublan?" Whitlaw asked, voicing a question that had been on his mind for the last thirty hours. "It was a lot closer to the ranch, and we might have gotten back to the States from there."

"My orders were to bring Missus Wright and her defenders to Babicora where she'd be safe for now. You and your

164

partner just happened to be there to help her, so we brought you along, too. Villa's reported to be in the Babicora area and two companies have been ordered up there."

Whitlaw sighed. He knew the Army's first priority was Villa. They were not in the business of transporting civilians—or, for that matter, rescuing women in distress.

"We were havin' a bit o' luck when we caught up with this train," Glasheen said. "I doubt my backside would've lasted another day on the leather-covered hickory o' that McClellan saddle."

"Everything works out for the best." Whitlaw nodded, recalling how the train had been delayed to gather wood for the boiler, allowing the mounted column to overtake it. Otherwise, they would still be struggling up and down this perpendicular country on horseback.

Maud Wright sat on a soldier's bedroll and leaned against the wall, cradling her daughter in a makeshift sling, fashioned from a shawl. She was soothing the infant with a canteen of sugar water, using a rag stopper for a nipple. She looked up and saw Whitlaw watching her. "I was away from the baby too long," she said. "My milk stopped flowing. I'm sure the fact that I was malnourished and dehydrated didn't help any."

"I didn't mean to pry," he murmured, feeling his cheeks getting warm.

"That's all right." She went back to trying to soothe the baby's hunger until they could reach the Hearst Ranch and obtain some proper food.

"Before we left Columbus, word was out that Carranza was furious over the invasion and had forbidden General Pershing to use the Mexican railroads," Whitlaw said to Captain Junius Bolt who was half squatting on a saddle to lessen the jolting of the car.

"Carranza doesn't know who he's dealing with," he replied

with a grim smile. "General Pershing was ordered not to use the rolling stock, but nobody mentioned the rails. So he telegraphed the general manager of the El Paso and Southwestern Railroad to send him a train from Texas. The general was determined to save wear and tear on both men and horses, if he could." Captain Bolt chuckled. "I was there, next day, when this train showed up. The general was fit to be tied when he saw the condition of this thing. A thousand hoboes must have hopped these cars over the last twenty years and built fires to keep warm. See those burn holes?" He pointed at the crude patches where boards had been hastily nailed to the floor nearby. "All the cars were like that. We would've had to shoot half the horses in the regiment with broken legs. Took the men two days to pull slats off the cars and tear down fences to cobble up enough patches. Also had to repack all the dry wheel bearings." He shook his head at the recollection. "They sent us a train that must have been on its way to the scrap yard. You'd think the El Paso and Southwestern management was in cahoots with the Carranza government!"

Whitlaw wondered how much of that off-hand remark might just be true.

"Then we got into the mountains and had to stop and wood up. Delayed for a day while the crew went on ahead with the locomotive and tender to find and chop enough wood to keep the boilers fired."

The lieutenant nodded. "At least that allowed our relief column to catch up."

If there was one thing Whitlaw had learned in his sixty-four years, it was to be patient and let events unfold. A man could avoid a lot of frustration if he didn't try to alter situations beyond his control. Military decisions were definitely beyond his control.

Creaking and swaying, the car jolted over the neglected roadbed. Whitlaw was grateful they were only crawling along or the ride would have been enough to jar their kidneys loose.

Three of Maud's six Mexican employees who'd forted up in the ranch house with her had opted to return to their homes. The remaining three were here on the train, seeking refuge with the U.S. military. One of the three, Ramón Carbajal, had kept to himself and remained virtually silent since they'd abandoned the ranch. He appeared to be in his early forties, with black hair, wind-burned olive skin, a flaring mustache beneath a beaked nose, and hazel eyes that were startling against the darker face. His appearance and demeanor would not have attracted Whitlaw's attention had it not been for the weapons he carried—a Krag-Jorgensen carbine and a web cartridge belt filled with .30-40 ammunition. Shoved under this belt was a double-action .38 nickel-plated Colt Lightning. Any Mexican who chose to wrangle horses for the *gringo* owners of the Wright Ranch would necessarily have to be well-armed. But this man did not look like a horse wrangler or ranch hand. The Krag had immediately piqued Whitlaw's curiosity.

In spite of the chill, the doors of the boxcar had been left open a foot to admit fresh air. Still, the atmosphere in the car was rank with unwashed bodies as well as the residual odors of previous cargoes.

After several minutes of silence, broken only by the clanking, lurching, and swaying of the car, Whitlaw remarked: "I believe I could walk faster than this. Think I'll go topside for some fresh air and scenery." He looked at Glasheen. "Coming?"

"This thing is bobbin' and weavin' worse than a ship in a seaway," he replied. "I believe I'll keep m'self anchored right here to this floor."

"I'll join you," Ramón Carbajal said, rocking forward away from the wall and onto his feet in one fluid motion. "I could use a smoke and don't want to bother the *señora* and the little one."

Whitlaw was startled at the words from this reticent man. "Glad for the company." He slid open the side door and caught his breath at the sight of the yawning, tree-studded chasm below. The train was rounding a sharp curve, and the black locomotive was *whoofing* a steady rhythm almost opposite their car, a hundred yards across the gorge.

He reached around to the iron rungs just outside. As he stepped out and swung himself upward, he had a fleeting thought that heights had never frightened him. Maybe he was meant to be a flyer, but born thirty years too soon.

Carbajal was right on his heels, and, in a few seconds, both men were seated on the catwalk atop the car. If Whitlaw thought this man would now begin to socialize, he was mistaken. The Mexican pulled out a short, briar pipe and began packing it with rough-cut tobacco. When he turned away from the slight breeze to cup a lighted match to the bowl, Whitlaw noted the long, slim fingers and manicured nails. Then he caught a whiff of the smoke. There was Latakia in the mixture. He got out his own pipe and tobacco.

The little things began to add up. This man was no ordinary peasant. In the States, Whitlaw would have guessed the small Colt, the slender, strong hands, the keen eyes, and reticence might have belonged to a gambler. If not that, then at least to a man of some refinement and education who was used to surviving in a hostile world. He wondered how this man happened to be defending Maud's ranch. Maybe if she was planning to stay in Mexico during all this turmoil after her husband was murdered, she'd been forced to fight fire with fire and hire men who could use weapons as handily as tools. No small group of peasant ranch hands could be expected to hold off marauding *Villistas,* or the other *bandidos* who roamed Chihuahua. He made a mental note to ask her.

The car lurched heavily and both men grabbed for the walkway to keep their balance. Up ahead, the black troopers whooped good-naturedly and fell against each other as their cars rocked and tilted.

Carbajal puffed thoughtfully on his pipe and stared off at the timbered slopes while the train continued to climb the pass.

Suddenly a *thumping* noise came from under the train. Then an agonized *screech* of metal, followed by the *spang* of snapping steel as a coupling broke. The two stock cars just ahead of them had gone off the rails and were bumping along the ties, tilting crazily. Their own car began to shake. A sudden jerk caught Carbajal off guard and he was flung down toward the edge of the roof.

In a blink, Whitlaw lunged and grabbed. He got a fistful of cloth and held on, gritting his teeth as the full weight of Carbajal's body yanked his arm. Whitlaw sprawled out, anchoring his lower half across the catwalk.

The twisting car ahead broke loose from their boxcar, and the two derailed stock cars tilted toward the precipice, then plunged down, one dragging the other. Screams of horses and falling troopers rang in the background of Whitlaw's mind as he struggled with all his strength, to keep his grip on the Mexican. Gasping, he managed to get his other hand on an ankle.

"Let go!" Carbajal yelled. "I can make it now!"

Whitlaw relaxed his grip and Carbajal disappeared over the edge, swinging himself into the open door below him.

169

Disconnected from the locomotive and the forward end of the train, the four boxcars and caboose stopped, and Whitlaw jumped up to grab the brake wheel before they began rolling backward. While he spun the wheel, the roar was beginning to subside as horses and shattered cars came to a sliding halt far below in the splintered trees and loose shale. Boards and hoofs and an upturned wheel truck were all he could distinguish in the clouds of dust that boiled up the mountainside.

Ten days later at the Hearst Ranch, Glasheen was looking out the spacious dining room window. "B'God, I believe it's beginning to snow!"

"Just a few late winter flurries. Nothing serious," Whitlaw answered, getting up and helping himself to another cup of coffee from the silver urn on the sideboard. He stood sipping the honey-sweetened brew and looking out at the white flakes whirling past the window. The human body and mind were capable of remarkable powers of recovery. Even a man as old as himself felt completely restored after ten days of proper food and rest in the Hearst ranch house, more a mansion. Seeing the military tents on the surrounding grounds, he couldn't help but feel sorry for the common soldiers who had to endure almost continuous hardships on this campaign. Eleven black troopers had been hurt in the train derailment. One of them had died within two hours. The others had various contusions, broken limbs, back injuries, and two complained of vague internal disorders. By some miracle, only the one man had been a casualty, although they had to shoot a number of horses. The crew recoupled the front half of the train to the remaining cars and made the injured men as comfortable as possible before the train continued on. However, Colonel William Brown, having seen all he wanted of trains, ordered his men to unload and saddle their horses. Whitlaw, Glasheen, Carbajal, and Maud Wright and her baby rode with them those last several miles over very rough country to the Hearst Ranch.

Having military rank, or being a civilian, had its privileges. Colonel Brown quartered officers and civilians inside the spacious ranch house, while the non-coms and enlisted men made do with tents and campfires on the acreage outside. They placed the injured troopers in two of the outlying guest cottages, where they were attended by two medics.

The gash on Whitlaw's scalp and the nicked ear were healing up nicely, while Glasheen's knees, although still sore, were functioning properly. His upper arm bullet wound, received in the raid on Columbus, was scabbed over and healing.

Whitlaw turned away from the window as Harvey Barcombe, the ranch manager, came into the room. He was a thick-set man with graying hair and had been a most congenial host. "Everybody get enough to eat?" he boomed.

A Mexican servant began clearing the late breakfast dishes. Glasheen snatched the last piece of bacon as the platter was going by. "Can't get enough o' that pig," he muttered, chewing.

"When is Mister Hearst due back?" Whitlaw asked.

"Can't rightly say. He usually wires us a couple of days ahead. He spends more time here in the summer, to enjoy the cool of the high mountains."

A telegraph wire ran to the Hearst ranch house and the military had been taking advantage of it instead of using the Signal Corp's balky wireless radios.

Maud Wright entered the room, and Whitlaw respectfully stood, an unconscious gesture of long habit.

"Just put the baby down for a nap," she said, accepting

171

the chair Glasheen held for her. "One of the servants was telling me Villa's been shot by one of his own men."

"Stuff and nonsense!" Barcombe snorted. "You wouldn't believe the rumors I've heard about that man, especially since the troops arrived. Our Mexican help is very good, by and large, but they pass along every piece of gossip as if it were gospel. Their relatives fill them with all kinds of tales. I've heard Villa has come in behind General Pershing to attack Columbus again. I've heard he's going after Carranza forces in Guerrero far to the southeast. I've heard he's been killed in an ambush and is secretly buried, so the *gringos* will think he's still alive. I don't know what to believe, so I don't countenance any of it. All I know for sure is that your troops came up here because someone said Villa was in this area, and he's not. Never has been." The big man paused to say something in rapid-fire Spanish to one of the servants, who bowed and departed. "It's more likely he's over toward the next valley, to the east," Barcombe continued. "But I understand Pershing has sent some troops in that direction, too."

"That's right, Mister Barcombe," Colonel Brown said, coming into the dining room at that moment. "And he's also dispatched Colonel Dodd with Custer's old outfit, the Seventh Cavalry, south from Dublan, to press as fast as tired horses can take them, to catch up with Villa. That is, in case he's headed south. Meanwhile, Lieutenant Foulois is trying to fly dispatches and orders between the various units, but those JN-Two's don't have the power to fly over the foothills, so they have to stay in the lower valleys." The colonel nodded to Maud Wright and accepted the cup of coffee Barcombe had drawn for him. "Barcombe," he said, sipping the steaming black brew, "we've imposed on Mister Hearst's hospitality long enough. It's apparent that Villa is

not around here. It's time we moved out and get these injured men to some proper medical attention. Some of their
broken bones have already started to heal crooked."

"I've been working on trying to arrange transportation
for them," Barcombe said. "But I'm having no luck getting
the Mexican authorities to let them ride the train to El
Paso. No reason. They just refuse."

"The official Mexican mind is beyond comprehension,"
Brown commented. "If we can figure out some way to carry
them on litters, maybe the injured can travel with the troop
when we move out."

"I've got an idea, Colonel," Barcombe said. "The rails
pass right along the edge of the estate. We have four hand
cars we use to go to town during winter snow or when no
buggy is available. With your permission, I'll transport the
injured down the mountain to Dublan on the hand cars.
Quicker, easier, and safer than going any other way."

"Best suggestion I've heard today," the colonel said,
draining his coffee cup.

"Beg pardon, sir."

"Yes?" Colonel Brown looked toward the vestibule and
returned the young lieutenant's salute.

"Telegram from General Pershing. Thought you'd want
to see it right away."

Colonel Brown took the proffered sheet, held it to the
light of the window, and was silent for several seconds while
he absorbed the message. "Just send an acknowledgment,
telling him the troop is moving out in the morning for
Dublan to await further orders. There are no *Villistas* here."

"Yes, sir!" The lieutenant saluted and left.

"General Pershing has just arrived in San Geronimo,
two hundred miles south of Dublan," Colonel Brown said.
"He rented a Dodge touring car from an American

Mormon settler there, who drove the general and his staff the whole distance. Several reporters were trying to keep up in Model-T Fords." He paused with a strange look on his face. "What has become of the cavalry?" he mused aloud. "Dodge touring cars for a moving headquarters? Reporters chasing along in Fords?" He shook his head in wonder, stuffed the telegram into his pocket, and stalked out of the room.

"Maud, are you going to stay here?" Whitlaw asked the young mother. "Glasheen and I are going with the injured to help pump the cars. We're anxious to get back to the border."

"Oh, I want to go with you!" she said firmly. "I've had all I can stand of this country for a while. I want my daughter to get a foothold in some stable place."

"Can I help you pack or get anything ready?"

"Packing is easy when you have nothing but the clothes you're wearing," she said, then smiled. "Actually, if you could see about some extra cow's milk to take along for the baby, I'd be grateful. It won't sour in this weather."

"Consider it done."

"I'll see if I can round up some cotton rags for diapers."

As he and Glasheen left the room, the Irishman was muttering something under his breath.

"What are you grumbling about?"

" 'Pray that your flight may not be in the winter or on the Sabbath. Woe be to them who have babes at the breast. . . .' "

"I think that rap you took on the head when we crash-landed has addled your brains. Besides, I think you've scrambled your Bible quotes."

"I'm going into the library to have a snort of Mister Hearst's brandy, then I'm going up to our room for a nap. If we're leaving early in the morning, I want m'body to have all the rest it can get."

"It's a little early for brandy, isn't it?"

"Never pass up a chance that may not come again. We'll be gone from here by this time tomorrow. Besides, it's goin' for midday . . . nearly eleven of the clock."

They entered the library. Glasheen hoisted a healthy shot he poured from a cut-glass decanter, sighed with pleasure, and left.

Whitlaw stayed behind in the library, enjoying the quiet and solitude of the moment, a temporary haven from war and revolution and turmoil. He wandered along the shelves, looking at the titles. William Randolph Hearst had accumulated a varied and extensive collection of books, many of them in Spanish. He couldn't tell how well used these books were, since the library was dusted daily by a housemaid. He pulled down an old copy of DON QUIXOTE, evidently in the original medieval Spanish. It was profusely illustrated. Whitlaw found himself wishing he could read it and appreciate the nuances of the original language. Something was always lost in translation, even with footnotes.

He heard the library door close softly behind him. "*Señor* Whitlaw?"

Startled from his reverie, he turned to see Ramón Carbajal standing there.

"May we have a word in private?"

Whitlaw nodded, replacing the volume on the shelf. There was nothing subservient in the man's manner—only dignified courtesy.

"You are the James Whitlaw who was accused of conspiring to steal a shipment of rifles two years ago." It was a statement, not a question, voiced in perfect English with almost no trace of an accent. "You are still trying to find out what happened to them."

"Why do you say that?" Whitlaw asked guardedly.

175

"One of the housemaids saw you in my room the other day, examining my Krag carbine. She came to me because she thought you were stealing from a poor Mexican. But I knew better."

Whitlaw could feel his face flushing with embarrassment.

"I suppose you wrote down the serial number."

Whitlaw did not answer.

"I have been studying you since that business at the Wright Ranch," Carbajal said, walking around the library table. "You and your friend came to rescue Maud Wright. That was very noble and brave."

"There's a little more to it than that," Whitlaw replied, waving off the compliment.

"Nevertheless, you came. Besides that, I am indebted to you for saving my life during that train derailment."

"I doubt the fall would have killed you."

"You are a man of principle and courage." Carbajal stood in a reflective attitude for several seconds, one hand on the back of a chair. "I have a proposition to offer. Even if you decline it, may I have your word as an honorable man that nothing of our conversation will leave this room?"

Whitlaw tried to neutralize his curiosity. "You have my word."

"I know where the guns are."

Chapter Fifteen

Whitlaw felt as if the man had just struck him in the solar plexus. "What? How . . . ?" His mouth went dry and his heart began to pound. He took a deep breath. "Where are they?"

"I can't tell you . . . I must show you."

"Why?"

"Nothing is free in this life, Mister Whitlaw. In exchange for taking you to these guns, I want half."

"Half?" Whitlaw's mind was in a whirl. How could he give this man half of what he didn't own? The guns were not his. If he were to locate them, it would be only for the purpose of clearing his own name, to show he had had nothing to do with their disappearance. Or, perhaps, he could tell the authorities that he'd found only half the shipment.

All this flashed through his mind as he stalled to absorb the sudden revelation. "Do you want the guns themselves, or half the money from their sale?"

"Either. I will turn the guns into money."

To hide the fact that his knees were getting too weak to hold him up, Whitlaw pulled out a chair and sat down at the small library table. For several seconds he remained silent, pondering the man's words. If Carbajal knew where the guns were, why didn't he just retrieve them, instead of offering to split?

"Why are you telling me this?"

"Because I need the help of an honest man to get them . . . someone who has an interest in finding them. You qualify on both counts. And I need a courageous man with a little money to help me transport them into Mexico."

"I have no money to speak of. How can I trust you? I know nothing about you."

"Then let me tell you a little about myself," Carbajal answered, beginning to pace around the room. "I'm a native of Chihuahua. My parents were able to give me a good education, and I became a young idealist, a firebrand, who was out to right all wrongs and save the world. I took up one cause after another, mostly concerned with the redistribution of land in Mexico, which entailed the overthrow of the dictator and the privileged landowners. I was one of an almost extinct group in this country . . . the middle class. I worked at a variety of jobs to support myself while I espoused various revolutionaries. Eventually I became the editor of a small newspaper. It gave me a wider voice and more influence, and I used it to make many political enemies with my editorials.

"I began to support Carranza, thinking that he, among all the competing factions, had the best chance of overthrowing Díaz. And most important, he had the ability to run a stable government. My only fear was that he might forget the peasants' claim to the land when he became president of all Mexico and had the ear of kings and presidents. As you well know, power corrupts." Carbajal paused with his back to Whitlaw and stared out one of the two library windows. A few flakes of snow were still drifting down in the still air outside.

Where was all this headed? Whitlaw waited and listened patiently.

"Three years ago I left my job at the newspaper and became a captain in the Carranza forces, fought several battles, and was wounded in the cause. A minor wound only, but one that served to remind me that I was not invulnerable. While I was recuperating . . . and because I was educated . . . I was assigned the task of negotiating with arms dealers from your side of the border. When Carranza's chances were still much in doubt, it was necessary that he get more arms. To make a long story a little shorter, the general manager of the El Paso and Southwestern Railroad offered to make a shipment of rifles available . . . for a price, and our help. . . ."

"Ah, so it *was* an inside job," Whitlaw interrupted.

Carbajal nodded. "We supplied the men who made it possible for this railroad official to divert the shipment of guns."

"And they let on that I was partially to blame!"

"You were a convenient scapegoat," Carbajal said. "The money changed hands, but the guns could only be hidden in a hurry. We were not able to get them across the border because, by then, the Villa forces had taken control of northern Chihuahua and we didn't want the rifles to fall into Villa's hands. As it turned out, Carranza didn't need those guns and has gone on to become the *de facto* president, while Villa, the ignorant *bandido,* remains only that . . . a bloody *bandido* who is intent on nothing but his own glory!"

A terrible bitterness was evident in the Mexican's voice when he spoke of Villa. Carbajal turned back to him and pulled up a chair on the opposite side of the table. "By this time I was older and had become somewhat disillusioned with the human frailties of even the best of revolutionary leaders. I wanted out of the struggle, and so took a job as a ranch hand and guard at the Wright Ranch. I was on an errand in Ascension the day Villa's men took the Wrights and killed *Señor* Wright two days later. Five other faithful hands and I protected her ranch for the week or two she was in the United States, and made sure the Mexican woman who was left with the baby took good care of the infant. I was overjoyed when Maud . . . *Señora* Wright . . . returned with the American troops. She is a remarkable woman," he said in an aside, his craggy face softening at the thought.

Whitlaw knew that Maud Wright meant more to him than just an employer.

"The Wright Ranch has been abandoned," Carbajal continued. "She is going to live in the States, so my job is ended. I, too, have grown tired of fighting and wish to make a fresh start in your country. I've done all I can for Mexico. It is time to move on. That's why I want the guns, or half the profits from them."

"How do I know there is any truth at all to your story?" Whitlaw asked, hardly able to countenance any of this.

"If you wrote down the serial number of my carbine, you know it is one of the stolen shipment."

Whitlaw had, indeed, written down the number, but had left his list of serial numbers in Columbus. "You could have gotten that gun anywhere," he said.

"True, but I didn't. It came directly from the shipment I helped hide."

"You call Villa a bandit. A man who steals a trainload of rifles must be called the same thing. And what happened to the train crew?"

Carbajal's face flushed darker; his lips compressed in sudden anger. "There was a time when I would have shot you for that remark. I am a patriot."

"One man's patriot is another man's bandit."

Carbajal seemed to have himself in hand again and went

on. "I am older and wiser now. I envy you because you are an honorable man. I admit that I have not always been so. But this is a practical matter. I have no money and now am unemployed. I need the money from those guns to make a fresh start in the United States . . . if a convicted felon can somehow become a citizen of your country."

"All right, I'll go along with your story, but why do you need my help? If you know where the guns are, why don't you go get them and take all the profits for yourself?"

"Because the guns are on your side of the border. And I don't know anyone else I can trust to help me."

"If I am an honorable man, what makes you think I will help you?"

"Because you want to clear your name, and I am the only one who is still alive who knows where they are hidden."

"I could hire somebody to kidnap the general manager of the El Paso and Southwestern Railroad."

"He had a stroke last month and remains in a coma, not expected to live."

Whitlaw tried to remember if he'd seen anything about this in the El Paso newspaper. He drew a blank.

"We need each other," Carbajal continued. "I have become a *persona non grata* in Chihuahua. The *Villistas* have put a price on my head. That is why I'm going down the mountain, tomorrow, on the hand cars to Dublan. From there, I will attempt to enter the States with or without your help."

Whitlaw hesitated. He could take this man at face value. He had to if he were to find out if Carbajal really knew the location of the rifles. "So, what do you want me to do?"

"You can either help me move the rifles, or you can pay me for my half."

"You must know I don't have that kind of money, unless I first find a buyer for my half."

"Then you will have to make arrangements for wagons or trucks to help transport them into Mexico."

This was becoming more and more bizarre. "How will you get into the States? Do you have a legal passport?"

"No."

Whitlaw thought for a moment. "Do you know anything about mechanics?"

"I have knowledge of many things. I can do some mechanic work."

"I'll talk the military into hiring you as a truck or airplane mechanic. We'll get you into Columbus that way."

"Then I'll see you in the morning," Carbajal said, rising and moving toward the door. He stopped with his hand on the knob. "Remember your promise to say nothing about this conversation."

"If I'm going to arrange to hire trucks and drivers to haul these weapons, I'll have to bring others into this," Whitlaw said with a shrug.

"We'll deal with that when we get to Columbus. The fewer, the better," he compromised. With cat-like movements, he was gone.

Whitlaw sat silently at the table. He would clearly have to cope with this in some way. And why had he promised not to say anything? Surely he would have to confide in Glasheen, who had a great interest in the guns. Glasheen had traveled all the way from Ireland to purchase them, only to find out the shipment was truly missing. Some of what Carbajal had said did not make sense to him. He shook his head and stood up. Maybe he had just sat down on the couch in the library and dozed off and dreamed this entire episode. After all, the rifles had been on his mind for many months. Yet, as he opened the door and went out of the library, he knew it had not been a dream. He would ponder it a while before he sought Glasheen's opinion.

The next morning, the five injured men who were unable to walk were carried on litters to a truck and loaded in with the other five, who were suffering from broken arms, ribs, and collar bones. They were driven the two miles to the edge of the Hearst Ranch, wrapped in blankets, and put aboard three hand cars. Carbajal, Barcombe, Whitlaw, and Glasheen, plus two Hearst Ranch employees, would operate the cars. Barcombe and the two workmen would return the three empty cars to the ranch later.

The two remaining Mexican defenders of the Wright Ranch had been hired by Barcombe as guards for the Hearst place, and stayed behind.

"We won't be meeting any trains on the way," Barcombe told them as they lined up to start. "None scheduled today." Then he shrugged. "But, knowing the Mexican authorities as I do, you never can tell. Keep your eyes open."

The party got under way shortly after daybreak. Whitlaw and Glasheen operated one car, while Carbajal and Barcombe shared pumping duties with two muscular men on the other two cars. Carbajal made sure Maud and her baby were aboard his car.

The day was uneventful. On the long downhill grade, they made good time, and the pumping was not arduous. The leaden overcast began to shed a heavier snowfall, making the evergreens appear to be dusted with powdered sugar.

They passed the spot where the derailment had occurred, and Whitlaw glanced down into the ravine where the remains of the shattered stock cars were beginning to blend into the rest of the landscape under a brushing of white. The stench of decaying horseflesh wafted the smell of death up the hillside, mingling with the fresh scent of pine.

Several of the injured black troopers pointed and spoke softly to one another as the cars rolled around the curve and toward the lower loop of the switchback.

The silent, snowy afternoon was pleasant, with nothing in sight but deep cañons covered with Mexican white pine, piñon, and locust. The only sounds were the long, metallic *shooooooooosh* of the steel wheels on steel rails, punctuated by the *clicking* over the rail joints. The heavy breathing of the men at the pump handles nearly drowned the smooth, sliding *whiiiiirr* of the greased gear wheels underneath.

By late afternoon, they had descended into the foothills, having covered fifty miles. Juniper, scrub oak, and ocotillo began to appear. Then the foothills gave way to grassy slopes dotted with saguaro, barrel, and yucca cacti as they rolled onto the desert. Sparrows flitted through the mesquite, and the plaintive call of a mourning dove could be heard, sounding a long way off. Whitlaw paused in his pumping and listened. When he was a boy, he'd known this bird as a "rain crow". Its mournful cooing brought back memories of long ago.

The air grew warmer at the lower altitude, but Whitlaw kept his leather jacket buttoned, since mountain snow had turned to valley rain. They pumped through Casas Grandes and on for another three miles to the Mormon settlement of Dublan where they finally stopped and unloaded.

The soldiers were quartered in Army tents, and more white-walled tents were erected for the civilians. Whitlaw resolved to get Maud Wright alone at the first opportunity to ask her about Carbajal. She would know more about him than anyone else in the party.

Everyone was given Army rations for supper—seasoned with hunger, since there had been no stop for lunch. The food was passable, but everyone agreed it didn't compare to the sumptuous fare they'd enjoyed at the Hearst Ranch.

After a day of continuous work at the pump handles, by dark Whitlaw and Glasheen were both ready for their blankets. Two cots in a canvas wall tent was not what they'd become accustomed to recently, but Whitlaw didn't care as he sat down and pulled off his shoes. The bursitis in his upper right arm had not bothered him when he was active and using his muscles. But now, as he sat quietly for a few minutes, his arm began to burn and tingle from shoulder to wrist. Nothing he couldn't live with—just one of the aggravations of getting older and the parts wearing out.

"Nice trip," Glasheen remarked, rubbing his knees now stiffened from too much riding and not enough walking.

"More work than flying, and not nearly as much fun," Whitlaw said.

"Thank the good Lord for that," Glasheen replied. "We wouldn't have survived much more fun." The Irishman stripped off to his under shorts and crawled wearily under his blanket. "A good night for sleepin'," he said, indicating the sound of rain drumming on the canvas overhead. "A little windier and I'd go t'sleep imagining I was home in County Kerry."

Whitlaw turned the lantern down and sat in the semidarkness, thinking. Should he go see if he could find Maud? He'd seen her and the baby at the mess tent earlier, but there were too many people around, including Carbajal, to have a private conversation. Besides, her baby had been fussy.

He rolled back on the cot and snuffed out the lamp

185

flame. No sense worrying about this business of the rifles. He was too tired to think any more about it today. " 'Sufficient is the day and the trouble thereof . . .'," he murmured by way of a prayer before he dozed off.

Whitlaw was mistaken if he thought they would be returned to the States via the Mexican rails to El Paso, or even by Army horse or truck to Columbus. At least it wasn't to happen for several days.

The contingent left behind by Pershing at Dublan had expanded and made camp more comfortable by adding wooden bases under their wall tents to help keep out bugs and mud. A few men had even built adobe walls, using the tent for a roof. Some innovative soldiers had pitched in and constructed a *jacal* with a sun-warmed rain barrel atop it for the purpose of taking a weekly shower. A cord pulled from inside opened a slot in the barrel to release water through a sieve. There were also other small luxuries soldiers can devise for themselves when they know they will be in one camp for several weeks.

Colonel Brown, the ranking officer, finally arrived with the rest of the cavalry, eager to get the injured home to Columbus for proper care. But he was hampered by the downpours that turned the desert roads into mush and sandy sinkholes. These had already proven they could mire down even the strongest truck.

Whitlaw took advantage of the delay to introduce Ramón Carbajal to Captain Weeks of the Quartermaster Corps. "One of the defenders of the ranch house," Whitlaw said. "He tells me he's a good mechanic. Thought you might like to put him on the payroll."

"That so?" The harried officer glanced up from supervising a private trying to adjust a carburetor of a Jeffery Quad truck.

"You know anything about Jennies? Lieutenant Foulois needs a mechanic badly to keep those things running."

Carbajal smiled. "I once listened to an OX-Five engine that was vibrating too much at low rpm's. Had the pilot shut it down, then took my pocket knife and whittled a few shavings off one end of the propeller blade. When we fired it back up, the engine was in perfect balance."

Captain Weeks looked at Whitlaw as if to verify this story.

Whitlaw shook his head. "I wasn't there."

"Well, I'll be satisfied if he can work on one of these mechanical beasts we have to haul supplies in." Weeks gestured at the truck with the hood cocked up on one side. Turning to Carbajal: "All right, you're hired. Let's see what you can do. We have to have four of these trucks ready to move out when the rain stops and the ground dries enough to support their weight. If the rain doesn't stop . . . well, Colonel Brown says we'll start day after tomorrow, regardless." He glanced at the weeping gray sky and shook his head.

Step one accomplished, Whitlaw thought as he set off to find Maud Wright while Carbajal was occupied, and Glasheen was taking a walk around the camp in the rain to exercise his knees. "Liquid sunshine," he'd said, smiling as he pulled down the brim of his hat and splashed away. "You forgot I work outside on the county roads. This feels like home."

Maud Wright occupied a tent the Army had graciously set aside for her and the child at the end of a row of identical white tents. He found her reading a novel borrowed from the Hearst library. The baby was asleep on the cot.

"Have you got a few minutes?" he asked, after announcing himself, then thrusting his head under the flap.

"Come in." She laid her book aside.

"What can you tell me about Ramón Carbajal?" he inquired, sitting cross-legged on the floor to let the water run off his leather jacket. "I understand he worked for you."

"That's right. My husband and I hired him more than a year ago. Not too good with stock, but we took him on more for his ability to use a gun than for other skills."

"That's what I suspected. Was he a newspaper editor before?"

"Said he was, although it was before we knew anything about him."

"How did you happen to hire him?"

"He rode up to the ranch one day and asked for a job. Said he was handy with tools, but had never done much ranch work."

"Did he tell you he'd fought for the Carranza forces?"

"He mentioned that. Said his life was on the line, and that some of Villa's men wanted to execute him. Apparently he'd done them more than a little damage."

"Do you think they were looking for him when the *Villistas* kidnapped you and your husband from the ranch?"

"*¿Quién sabe?* They'd never bothered us before. Ramón was in town that day on some errand. Maybe the *Villistas* were frustrated and took us instead. But I think they were just a mean bunch who were out to hurt some *gringos*."

She stopped and looked at him carefully. "Why are you so interested in this man?"

"He made me a business proposition, and I wanted to find out a little about his character and background. Did he ever appear dishonest or vengeful?"

She paused, pursing her lips. "To live in this country as we did for several years, you have to be a good judge of character. I was better at it than my husband. Call it woman's intuition." She smiled slightly. "Vengeful . . . yes.

188

Dishonest . . . no. He has a hard, mean streak beneath that surface gentility. I certainly wouldn't want to cross him. But he was a man of his word. You may not like what he said or did, but he was true to his word, every time."

"Thank you, Missus Wright. That tells me what I need to know. Is there anything about him I should know that you haven't mentioned?"

"First of all, it's Maud, not Missus Wright." She smiled at him. "Nothing that I can think of. I'll just say he's a good man to have on your side in a fight to the death. Several times his shooting accuracy kept us from being overrun, even though we were badly outnumbered."

"You know," Whitlaw said, getting up, "I'm surprised they didn't try to fire the house."

"I think they wanted the house intact to use for themselves. After all, there's a spring nearby that feeds a small creek. That house would make a good way station for their troops." She stood up with him as he opened the tent flap. "I know I've thanked you more than once for coming to help when we really needed it. Bullets from the sky was the last thing those *Villistas* expected. And, from all indications, you did them considerable damage after you came down, too." She encircled his neck with an arm and kissed his stubbly cheek.

To cover his sudden embarrassment, Whitlaw said: "Better not let Carbajal see you doing that. I think he's sweet on you."

"What?" She seemed genuinely startled.

"Sometimes the people closest to you are the least obvious. Just a word to the wise," he said, dropping the tent flap behind him and putting on his hat against the drizzle.

Chapter Sixteen

It was more than a week after they arrived on the hand cars before Colonel Brown decided he'd had enough delays and started the four-truck convoy north, escorted by a detachment of cavalry.

Just before they left, a wireless message was received from Parral, more than 400 miles deep into Mexico, that Major Tompkins and the 13th Cavalry had been fighting a running battle with Carranza forces.

Another message brought the disturbing news that General Pershing had been fired on. He and his headquarters company, consisting of several autos and a truck, carrying mechanics with spare parts for the Jennies, had been attacked, but rallied and drove off their attackers.

As yet, no one had set eyes on Pancho Villa—the object of all this. And why were U.S. troops fighting Carranza forces?

"Why? Because Carranza does not want American troops in his country, no matter who they say they're chasing," Glasheen said when he and Whitlaw discussed it after breakfast as they made ready to depart. "Pride is one o' the seven deadly sins," Glasheen went on, wiping his mouth. He stuffed a biscuit with bacon into the side pocket of his dirty leather jacket. "And pride seems to be at the very top o' this Carranza's list."

"Villa is not the common enemy," Whitlaw said. "In spite of his being a brutal bandit, many of the peasants look upon him as some sort of folk hero, a Mexican Robin Hood, to be protected and hidden from the invading *gringos* who have come charging south with all their weapons and trucks and planes."

"As you Yanks say . . . I think you've hit the nail on the head." Glasheen grinned.

Whitlaw was not surprised to see Carbajal maneuver himself into the same truck with Maud Wright and her child. Whether or not she would develop any romantic interest in this man was none of Whitlaw's business. Unless she asked for his help, he would stay clear of the issue. Whitlaw had avoided the man during their enforced stay in Dublan. The conversation in the library seemed to have taken place weeks ago, and Whitlaw had kept the details in his mind, trying to recall exactly what the Mexican had said, trying to decide if he'd actually told the truth about the rifles.

Whitlaw was still arguing with himself about whether he should tell Glasheen now. At some point he would have to, since he would need his help to salvage the shipment if, indeed, it was still intact.

The trucks and cavalry started north. What appeared from the vantage point of an airplane to be a flat, dun-colored valley was, in reality, a gently rolling, sandy terrain, cut up by washes from the recent rains. Most of the time, the loaded trucks whined and groaned in their lower gears, often becoming mired in the soft soil. The rain continued off and on for the first several hours. Toward sundown, the sky cleared, and they found firmer sand to roll on. They decided to push forward into the moonlit night as long as they could. Around midnight the convoy halted, and the mounted column formed a cordon around the parked trucks, as if protecting a wagon train. The late supper was only cold rations, since there was no wood for cooking fires and what brush was available was too wet to burn.

The second full day on the road was long and exhausting. One truck punctured an oil pan on a sharp rock. They discovered the leak before the engine burned up, made temporary repairs, and replenished the oil. After considerable delay, the entourage got under way and went only five miles in less than an hour before another heavily loaded truck bogged down trying to cross a wash that looked deceptively dry. It was unloaded and another truck was chained to its axle to pull it out. Driving with a heavy load in sand caused two of the radiators to boil over, and the convoy had to halt until the engines cooled enough to continue. Finding standing water was no problem. They scooped it up by the bucketful from the hollows and strained it through an undershirt to filter out sand and grit before pouring it into the radiators or using it for washing. They carried water sufficient for cooking and drinking in small barrels on board.

The road had been grooved and eroded by run-off of spring rains and, when dry, blown away in dust storms. With the exception of the mounted cavalry, able-bodied men walked more than they rode in the trucks. Maud Wright, when she wasn't tending her baby, insisted on doing her share of walking to lighten the load on the vehicles. The road was rugged and slow, but not mountainous, or they could not have made it in the trucks. Whitlaw was amazed that the distance they'd covered in his Jenny in less than an hour took two and a half days by road. The future of travel was in the air.

On the second day, an hour before dark, they finally rolled and walked the last mile across the border into

Columbus. The terrain looked the same, but the crossing of that invisible line gave Whitlaw a feeling of lightness and freedom. It was good to be home!

As soon as they halted on the Camp Furlong parade ground, a sergeant in the Quartermaster Corps had Carbajal removing and cleaning the spark plugs from one of the straight-eight engines.

Whitlaw and Glasheen took advantage of his absence to escort Maud Wright to supper at the one remaining hotel.

"B'God, look there!" Glasheen exclaimed as they passed through the hotel lobby.

"What's that?"

Whitlaw and Maud followed his pointing finger toward a wall calendar behind the registration desk.

"Today's Easter Sunday and we haven't even been to church!"

"There's no church of any kind in Columbus," Whitlaw reminded him.

"More's the pity!" Glasheen lamented as they passed on into the adjoining dining room. "If I stay here long enough, I'll become a heathen, sure!"

After supper they made sure that Maud and her child were safely ensconced in a hotel room. Over her objections, Whitlaw paid a week's rent until other arrangements could be made.

The two men retired wearily to their adobe, swept out the spider webs, lighted a coal-oil lamp, and brought out their pipes for a smoke before turning in.

"I never thought I'd be homesick for the likes of this place," Whitlaw said, blowing a cloud of smoke at the ceiling. "But I'm glad t'be back."

"A tiny bit o' heaven after what we've been through," Glasheen agreed, shoving tobacco into his pipe bowl with a stubby thumb. "I'll have t'say, though, that Mister Hearst keeps a right tidy little place, stocked with all the comforts o' home."

"We could do the same if we had that kind of money," Whitlaw said. He leaned back in his chair by the kitchen table and crossed his legs. "And, speaking of money, do you still have that letter of credit at the bank?"

"That I do, for all the good it does me."

"You'll have to draw on it if you take the train to El Paso to buy a truck . . . one that will carry at least two tons."

"Now what would I be needin' with a lorry that size?"

"To haul about half the rifles you came here to get."

Glasheen paused, a lighted match halfway to the pipe bowl, and stared at Whitlaw, wide-eyed. Then he chuckled and applied the match to the tobacco. "I'm too tired tonight for the jokes, m'lad," he said between puffs.

"This is not a joke. Prop your feet up on that chair and give a listen. Then you can decide if what I'm about to say is true."

Whitlaw proceeded to relay everything Carbajal had told him, and then the information Maud had shared about the man.

Glasheen pondered the tale for a long minute while puffing on his pipe. "There's an odor o' rotten mackerel about it," he finally said. "Is he the only one who knows where the guns are? If so, what happened to the others? If not, why didn't someone else connected with this revolution try t'retrieve them during the two years since they went missing? And why is he offering t'split the shipment with ye?"

"I don't know the answer to the first two questions. As to the latter, he claims he needs my help to transport them. I suppose he's broke."

Glasheen shook his head. "If he'd actually negotiated

with the El Paso gunrunners and the general manager of the railroad, he has connections to the wealthy and powerful. A man like that would have no trouble obtaining money, or the help of men with money. Why would he offer to give you half, if he could arrange to take it all for himself?"

"He'd have to pay whoever he gets, and he selected me because . . . to quote him . . . I'm 'courageous and honorable'. I guess he's tired of dealing with crooks. He said the Carranza faction had paid for the stolen shipment but were unable to transport it across the border because the *Villistas* had control of northern Chihuahua then. Now he claims he wants to start a new life in the States, if he can somehow become a citizen in spite of his felony record."

"Crossing the right palms with silver will usually take care o' that," Glasheen said.

"That's a way of life in Mexico . . . I'm not so sure about this country."

" 'Tis not our problem," Glasheen said. "Come morning, I'll hit the bank, then start for El Paso. Even a lorry that could haul two and a half tons would not come near carrying half the shipment. I believe there's in the neighborhood of four thousand weapons, plus considerable ammunition."

"That's right," Whitlaw said. "Each carbine weighs eight pounds, each rifle about ten. They're packed six to a case. So each case weighs about sixty to sixty-five pounds. Let's see . . . a truck that can carry five thousand pounds could haul a maximum of . . . just over eighty cases, or approximately five hundred guns, not counting any cases of cartridges. We'd need five trucks to carry off half that shipment, or at least five trips in one truck. How were you originally planning to get those rifles to Ireland?"

"I was t'send an encoded wireless message to San Juan,

Puerto Rico for the captain of an Irish freighter t'meet me at the port o' Galveston . . . there, the cases would be loaded as farm implements and parts." He shrugged. "I've had t'notify him t'go ahead on his regular run to Argentina for now."

Whitlaw nodded. "Well, as improbable as this tale sounds, I think we need to follow up and find out where he'll lead us."

"Revolution breeds duplicity," Glasheen said. "One must tell lies t'cover previous lies. Once started, there's no end to it. If we follow this Carbajal, we'd best go armed and watch each other's back. If he's as good with a gun as you say he is, we must be on our mettle."

Whitlaw thoughtfully tamped the fire in his pipe bowl with the head of a nail. "Maybe you'd better hold off going to El Paso. Before we start acquiring trucks and making any long range plans, we need to be shown the rifles. If they exist, then we'll have a better idea of what to do next."

"Agreed."

"If that shipment is still intact, then you and I can discuss the matter of legal ownership."

Glasheen smiled. "B'God, as far as I can see, the laws o' salvage apply, right enough. The U.S. government got paid for a load o' surplus weapons by the California buyers, the California buyers got paid by the insurance company for the loss, the robbers got paid by the Carranzas who then didn't take delivery. Finders, keepers."

"Wouldn't they belong to the insurance company that paid for them?"

"The insurance company is in the business of gambling on winning or losing. They win when they continuously collect premiums and no claims are made. They have many more wins than losses, or they couldn't stay in business. Besides, they've probably figured out a way t'defray their taxes based on their so-called losses. No, it seems t'me . . . and I've looked at it from every angle . . . that these rifles are like a sunken Spanish treasure ship . . . regardless o' where the gold came from initially, it now belongs t'whoever finds it."

"Of course, that doesn't take into account the lives of the train crew."

"Assuming they're dead, it's regrettable. But, like the crews o' the Spanish galleons who went down with their gold in a hurricane, the loss o' life in no way affects the treasure . . . the rifles."

Since Ramón Carbajal was technically in the employ of the Army, he was allowed to sleep in one end of the enlisted men's barracks where he could be called for mechanical emergencies or breakdowns, day or night. There were three other mechanics on the civilian payroll, but the Mexican chose not to associate with them.

The next morning, Whitlaw and Glasheen gave an oral report to Colonel Slocum on the results of their air-rescue mission. He had already heard bits and pieces from Colonel Brown and was eager to get a detailed, first-hand account. Slocum gave his orderly strict instructions that he was not to be disturbed except in an emergency, then sat the two men down in armchairs in his office, leaned back behind his desk, and listened to their tale, now and then interrupting with a question.

"By God! That's one helluva story! Wait till it hits the papers."

The two men looked at each other. "Maybe that's not a real good idea," Whitlaw said. "We did you a favor by going. Now I want you to do us a favor by keeping all this quiet. Or, if you do give out the story, just say it was two anonymous civilians who don't want to be identified."

"Why?"

"Can't say just now. Personal reasons."

"Well, if that's the way you want it. . . ." Colonel Slocum was plainly disappointed. Then he brightened. "That might not be a bad idea, after all . . . it'll lend an air of mystery to the whole affair. And it won't hurt my career one bit, when my superiors in Washington find out I had the good sense to arrange for civilian volunteers to go rescue an American widow . . . and save the military the time and expense." He beamed a benign air of satisfaction that was somehow out of character. "Can I do anything for you boys? Get you anything? Is it too early for a drink or a cigar?"

They both declined with thanks. Whitlaw sneaked a look at his watch.

"Well, then there are other matters I must attend to," the colonel said, taking the hint. "Just be glad you're not under my command, so you don't have to make out a written report of this trip." He grinned. "I'm sorry about the loss of your Jenny."

"Easy come, easy go," Whitlaw said. "Maybe I'll come into some money and buy another airplane."

The two men shook hands with the colonel and left the office. As they crossed the parade ground, they recognized Carbajal from the back, bent over the side of a truck engine.

"Ramón!"

His head came up.

"We'll meet you for lunch at noon in the hotel."

Carbajal nodded curtly and went back to work. Maybe he was telling the truth about knowing something of mechanics. So far, at least, he had the Army fooled.

Two hours later a hastily washed Carbajal, smelling of

sweat and grease, met them in the hotel dining room. The three men were able to find a corner table to themselves.

"I can't stay long. We've got a transmission torn down."

The waiter appeared and the Mexican ordered a sandwich and a bottle of beer to go. The waiter took the other orders and left.

"We've got to see this shipment before I make plans about helping you move it," Whitlaw said in a low voice.

"I expected that. Rent a wagon or buggy and meet me at ten o'clock a half mile west of the depot, along the railroad tracks."

"We'll be there. Anything else?"

"No." In contrast to the worldly, confident attitude he'd displayed in the Hearst library, Carbajal seemed nervous, distracted. He didn't meet their eyes, and kept glancing at other customers in the room.

The waiter brought their food, and Carbajal stood with his sandwich and beer in a sack. "I'll pay you later."

"What's your hurry?" Whitlaw asked. "You're not a real mechanic who has to depend on that job for a living."

Carbajal only gave them a blank look and walked out.

"Something's amiss," Glasheen said, digging into his mashed potatoes.

"Or something's missing . . . between the ears," Whitlaw said. "I don't know which is the real Carbajal . . . the urbane, cocky gunman I met a few days ago, or this guy who acts like a rabbit in front of a hunter. I'm beginning to suspect he has a mental problem."

Changing the subject, Glasheen said: "Colonel Slocum was so elated, he didn't even ask for our .45's back."

"I know. Cheap enough payment for what we did."

"I've still got a couple extra full clips for mine."

"Good. Bring them tonight."

"Did you check the serial numbers o' those Krags against the list o' stolen weapons?" Glasheen asked.

"Yes. The one I got during the raid was not one of them, but the carbine Carbajal has *is* one of the stolen shipment."

Glasheen gave him a quizzical look.

"I know. It doesn't add up to anything. As I told Carbajal, he could have gotten that weapon anywhere."

"What did he say about your telling me this story, after he swore you t'secrecy?"

"I said if he wanted me to help him, I had to bring you in because you had the money to buy a couple of trucks. I never mentioned that you have an interest in the rifles yourself."

That afternoon Whitlaw went to the town's only livery and rented a buckboard and team of stout mules, mentioning in an offhand way that he had to haul some lumber. The buckboard was cheap and would get them wherever they were going.

He arrived back at the adobe, unhitched the mules, and tethered them on the shady side of the house, away from the oleander bush. Then he pumped a bucket of drinking water for them.

He rinsed off his hands and came into the house. Glasheen was sitting at the table, a stricken look on his face.

"What's wrong? You sick?"

Glasheen merely turned the El Paso newspaper around and pointed at the headlines:

IRISH UPRISING CRUSHED
British Troops Quell Easter Sunday Rebellion
Bloodshed in Dublin
GPO Site of Fierce Fighting

The column continued, giving further details of the bloody conflict in the heart of the city, the gunfire around the General Post Office. The rest of the country had failed to rise up in unison and join those who'd lit the fuse on Sunday morning.

"I can't believe it," Glasheen said, his voice choking. Tears filled his eyes. "All that planning, all that preparation . . . for nothing."

"Maybe it's not as bad as they make it out to be," Whitlaw consoled. "You know how newspapers tend to make even the most minor incidents sensational."

"If even half of this is true, the rising has failed." He shook his head sadly. "The leaders have already been jailed by the British."

Whitlaw didn't know what to do or say. Glasheen was inconsolable.

"The piece continues on an inside page," Glasheen said. "The Germans sent a ship, loaded with Mausers and disguised as a Norwegian freighter. It cruised around the north of Ireland and down the coast to rendezvous off the southwest tip at Kerry. Somehow, they missed the signal o' their contact, or got the wrong bay, or something. The German captain waited twenty-four hours, then proceeded around the southern coast toward home. A British destroyer forced him t'divert into Queenstown harbor for inspection. The German captain scuttled his ship at the mouth o' the harbor t'keep the guns out o' British hands." Glasheen shook his head. "The whole scheme was too complicated from the beginning. Not even all the leaders were united in insisting the rising should go forward. Most Irishmen are good fighters, but I can't blame them for not joining in, if they didn't have the full support of the leadership and some guns t'fight with."

"Since the rising failed and the German Mausers were lost, you won't have any need for those Krags," Whitlaw said.

"On the contrary. This struggle isn't over yet. I'm much afraid some o' the leaders will be hanged as an example to the others. They will be heroes, even if their judgment was faulty." He paused with a faraway look in his eyes. "We've been trying t'buck off British domination for centuries. If I can get those Krags into Ireland and distributed, the volunteers will be armed for the next round. We'll go underground and fight a guerrilla war like the Sinn Fein wanted t'do from the beginning."

Whitlaw saw the muscles of the Irishman's jaw work as he clenched his teeth in silent determination. Then he blinked a tear away and cleared his throat. "Who knows? If I had gotten those Krags sooner, the outcome might have been different."

"I'm convinced nobody really controls history," Whitlaw said. "Sometimes we can nudge it this way or that, but it keeps rolling along its own path, like some ponderous wheel."

"Then I'll do a bit of nudging tonight," Glasheen said, reaching for the holstered Colt automatic hanging on the back of a chair.

"I wouldn't be getting my hopes up, if I were you," Whitlaw said. "I'm still leery of Carbajal's story. There may not be any Krags at all."

"Then what would be his motivation?"

"Maybe he's luring us into a trap to be killed by the *Villistas.*"

"What?" Glasheen scoffed. "He is after fighting the Villa bunch at the ranch!"

"In spite of his claims that he's an idealist, a man like

Carbajal is a mercenary. I have him pegged as a gunman who'll work for whoever pays him. We shot down a bunch of *Villistas*. Someone may be paying him to get us."

Glasheen shook his head. " 'What a tangled web we weave . . . ,' " he started to quote. "We'd best be ready for anything tonight."

Chapter Seventeen

"Whoa!"

Whitlaw drew rein on the span of mules and brought the wagon to a creaking halt near the railroad tracks. He peered into the darkness. A heavy overcast blanketed the sky. Whitlaw was far-sighted and needed his glasses only for reading or close work, but he slipped them on anyway. They didn't help. He guessed they were more than 800 yards west of the last lights in the depot.

"Where is he?" Glasheen asked after several seconds.

"Dunno. We might be a little early."

"Maybe we should light the lantern."

"If this is an ambush, that's just what he'd want."

They sat silently for five more minutes, the only sound a soft ripping noise as the mules took advantage of the stop to tear at the sparse grass.

"Whitlaw?" A cautious voice came from the blackness.

"Yeah. Come ahead."

The *crunching* noise of steps approached through the rock ballast. "I was a ways up the tracks. Thought I heard the mules," came Carbajal's voice.

"I got a buckboard. All they had," Whitlaw said as the Mexican's form appeared out of the murk.

"Bueno." Carbajal stepped on a wheel hub and into the back of the buckboard. "Let's go."

"Which way?"

"Straight west. Follow along the north side of the right of way."

Whitlaw was uneasy with the Mexican behind him, but didn't want to show it by suggesting Glasheen change places. He snapped the reins, and the mules leaned into their traces. The wagon lurched forward.

As his eyes grew accustomed to the dark, Whitlaw could sense the slight rise of the rail bed to his left. "How far?" he asked over his shoulder.

"Until I say stop," Carbajal replied shortly. "Put the mules into a trot. We have a ways to go yet."

"Hyah!" Whitlaw popped the lines and the animals picked up the pace to a trot. The loose-jointed buckboard rattled and bounced along the uneven ground through the low desert shrubs. They were making about fifteen miles an hour. Whitlaw wondered what the unseen cacti were doing to the mules' legs.

There was no more conversation for the next twenty minutes, until Whitlaw slowed the team to a walk. "Give 'em a little breather," he said.

After ten minutes, he again whipped them up to a trot. He repeated this twice more, then said: "They'll have to have water soon. They've been working for over an hour."

"There's a water tank a little way up ahead," Carbajal said.

Whitlaw remembered having seen the water tower from the air when he and Glasheen flew this way the day they ran into the storm. Considerable rain had fallen so far in April and was threatening to start again. Lightning flickered in the distance. A metal bucket hung under the wagon, but Whitlaw had planned on the mules just drinking from rain water still standing in puddles.

They reached the water tank. Carbajal climbed the wooden structure and pushed on the counterbalanced spout until Whitlaw could grab the cord to pull it down. Water gushed into the bucket, and the mules drank their fill.

"Only a quarter mile farther," the Mexican said, dropping back into the buckboard.

While Whitlaw drove the mules at a walk, he had the strange feeling they were bound for the very place he and Glasheen had been set to explore the day they were diverted to Mexico. His suspicions were confirmed when Carbajal told him to stop the wagon and light the bull's-eye lantern. Whitlaw climbed down and tethered the mules by the long lines to a nearby mesquite bush. Carbajal took the lantern and led them along the tracks several yards, evidently looking for something.

"Here." He stopped. Whitlaw saw that the lantern light exposed spike holes in the ties and the marks showing something had once been there. "The switch was removed," Carbajal said. "Bring up the wagon."

Whitlaw did as instructed, and the three men climbed back aboard. Carbajal held the lantern over the side and guided them, while Whitlaw drove the team at a walk. They were following the traces of the absent railroad spur they'd seen from the air. The different colored earth and scuffed soil was not as obvious by lantern light as by daylight. But, now and then, Whitlaw could detect the signs. In this uncertain light, even a good tracker would have to know what to look for. The casual observer would never have noticed it.

The mules moved at a deliberate walk and the wagon followed, illuminated in the small circle of jiggling light.

By Whitlaw's estimate, they'd traveled nearly a mile when Carbajal called a halt. "Stay here for now." He got down and proceeded on foot. The lantern, swinging this way and that, illuminated the Mexican's booted legs as he searched for the trail. Daylight would have been a great help, since even the traces of absent rails could not vary much—perhaps a gentle curve. It was easy to lose one's bearings in the dark. Also, creosote bush, mesquite, and yucca appeared to have grown on the former rail bed.

"We would've been here ourselves if we hadn't gone off on that wild escapade to Mexico," Glasheen said in a low voice.

"Right. But we wouldn't have known what we were looking for . . . he does."

"I don't trust him," Glasheen muttered. "He's wearing a full cartridge belt and pistol and carrying that carbine. Is that for protection against us?" He sounded incredulous.

"Wish I knew. Just be alert."

The lantern had receded several hundred yards. A flicker of lightning in the distance briefly silhouetted the desert mountain less than a mile in front of them. The night air was close and sultry. Desert heat would be intolerable if the humidity stayed this high. But the April rains had brought at least one benefit—desert wildflowers were blooming in profusion. Poppies, primroses, asters, desert sunflowers, and at least a dozen others he couldn't name. He enjoyed them during their brief appearance.

"Is he signaling?" Glasheen asked, interrupting Whitlaw's musing.

The pinpoint of light was swinging in a rhythmic circle, over and over, as if gesturing.

Whitlaw popped the reins and the team jerked into motion.

Ten minutes later they were nearing the lantern; the bulk of the mountain, looming up, blocked out much of the frequent sheet lightning.

"Go slow and I'll guide you," Carbajal said, walking near the off-side mule, studying the ground while he moved along. His carbine hung by its leather sling across his back, out of the way.

Whitlaw noticed trickles of blood low on the mules' legs. Likely a brush with catclaw or *cholla*.

"Hold it." The Mexican went forward alone, the lantern swinging back and forth, searching. The light picked up yellow and white flowers growing in the crevices of the jumbled gray lava flow. The light was suddenly diffused by a thicket of mesquite, then partially blocked by a rock outcropping, then nearly disappeared into the mountain. Only a tiny shaft of reflection escaped the confines of the rock cleft.

"Where'd he go?" Glasheen whispered, sounding oppressed by the blackness and remote solitude of the desert night.

The light reappeared and its bearer made his stumbling way back to the wagon. "This is it. *Vamanos.*"

Whitlaw and Glasheen climbed down on opposite sides. Whitlaw secured the mules by their long reins to a stout paloverde. With one hand on the flap of his holster, he followed the bobbing light, cursing softly as he raked his shin against a sharp rock. Glasheen labored along in his wake.

"B'God! What's that?" Glasheen jumped, bumping Whitlaw.

The beam of the bull's-eye lantern swung around to illuminate a whitened skull in a clump of *cholla* spines. Tusks jutted from the elongated jaw.

"Javelina," Carbajal said. "The desert claims its own." He resumed his lead.

Whitlaw let Glasheen go ahead of him, since he seemed nervous bringing up the rear. Whitlaw looked over his shoulder before following them into a thick clump of mesquite. Suddenly he stopped. A tiny shaft of light flashed for an instant, and then was gone. He caught his breath and waited for it to reappear. Straining his eyes for several seconds brought no reward—only blackness. Perhaps he'd imagined it. Possibly distant lightning reflecting off a piece of mica. But it had been too bright for that. Some unexplained oddity of this desert land, like the glow of foxfire in the Eastern woodlands, or the atmospheric electricity of St. Elmo's fire. Yet, a chill swept over his sweat-damp back as he hurried to catch up with the receding lantern.

"Whitlaw?"

"I'm here." Dragging himself upward by pulling on mesquite bushes, he struggled up a pile of shattered stone and finally reached a giant fissure in the rock, several yards wide. Looking skyward, he saw that the lantern light barely reached the top of the upthrust slabs that formed the walls. The broken and seamed rock walls leaned toward each other, leaving a small slot of open sky more than a hundred feet above his head. Whitlaw knew little about geology, but the mountain seemed to be composed of granite and cooled cinders of lava, mixed together, shading from dark gray to a light coffee color. From the marks of metal tools on the rock, and boulders blasted loose from the walls, he figured men had attempted to mine something here in years past—maybe copper or silver.

They were still moving slowly when Glasheen suddenly stopped and Whitlaw ran into him. Carbajal stood in front of them and swung the beam of the bull's-eye lantern toward a jumbled pile of rock ahead. "*Señores,* there is the trainload of weapons!"

At first Whitlaw saw nothing. Then the light picked out an iron coupling protruding from the pile of shattered rock. He caught his breath.

"We will climb over," Carbajal said. "Step where I step." He held the lantern low so they could see only his legs along the pile of man-made scree. Panting, slipping, sliding, they struggled up the loose pile that was a good twenty feet high. Clouds of fine rock dust boiled up into the lantern light and stuck to their sweating skin.

"It is just as I last saw it!" he said, holding the light high once they all stood atop the rock fall. They were actually standing almost on top of a red caboose. As the Mexican swung the lantern forward and the light reflected from the pale rock walls, Whitlaw saw two boxcars and the cab of a locomotive. The train was buried several feet up its sides, giving all the appearance of being trapped in a North Dakota snowdrift. But here, its prison was heaps of broken rock, not snow. Several inches of rock dust coated the tops of the cars.

"We can climb down alongside this last car where the door was forced open," Carbajal said, leading the way and using the butt of his carbine as a walking stick to steady himself.

The two men joined him at the open side door. He flashed his light inside, and they stepped in between two rows of wooden crates. Whitlaw pulled a thick-bladed sheath knife from his belt and thrust it under the lid of the nearest. He wiggled and pried, working loose the nails, and lifted one end of the lid. Three long Krag-Jorgensen rifles lay cradled upside down in the notches of wooden racks, and three more lay beneath. He put away his knife, grabbed one of the weapons, and wiped off the thick lubricant with a bandanna. "Well preserved. No rust," he commented. "All new?"

"About half new from the Springfield Armory and half used from other arsenals," Carbajal said. "Although I didn't have time to examine them." The Mexican swung the lantern around. The forward half of the boxcar was filled with similar cases; the aft half was stacked nearly to the ceiling with metal ammunition boxes.

"B'God, in the hands of our volunteers, this might have turned the tide in Dublin!" Glasheen breathed, obviously impressed.

"I'm finally seeing what I was accused of stealing," Whitlaw said. "What about the crew?"

Carbajal motioned them outside. Whitlaw replaced the rifle in the open case and followed him back up the entrapping rocks to the top of the train.

The men walked along the tops of the cars to the engine. There, the light flashed on three dusty corpses, lying where they'd fallen more than two years earlier. Whitlaw had to choke down his anger. He climbed over the coal in the tender and down into the small cab. Carbajal handed him the lantern. The engineer, fireman, and a third man he took to be one of the guards lay as they had been executed. Two years of exposure had deteriorated the bodies, but not to the extent he expected. They were shrunken and shriveled, mummified by the dry air. Brown, leathery skin stretched over the dried-out muscles, giving them a gaunt look, as if they had starved to death. The flesh was gone from the tips of their noses and their lips, exposing their teeth in what appeared to be a ghastly grin at this whole situation. The footplate was sprinkled with dry rodent droppings as if kangaroo rats or mice had gnawed on the ragged clothing and some of the missing tissue.

"Where are the brakemen and the guard?"

"In the caboose."

Whitlaw, clad in only a light wool jacket, was sweating more than usual, even though the dead air inside this mountain was relatively cool. He felt slightly sick at his stomach and could taste the beef and chile peppers he'd eaten for supper.

Whitlaw handed up the lantern, then pulled himself up the ladder to the top of the tender. Suddenly tired, he sat down on the roof of the first boxcar. "All right, before we discuss moving this cargo, how about you telling me just what happened." He positioned himself cross-legged and, as if for comfort, slid his gun belt around so the loosened flap of the holster would leave his Colt automatic within easy reach, should he need it in a hurry.

But Carbajal seemed relaxed. He laid down the carbine and pulled a *cigarillo* from his shirt pocket. The match flared and he cupped it to his smoke, revealing the hawk nose and hooded eyes in his dark face.

Glasheen silently moved off to one side at the edge of the light.

"Here is the story from the beginning," Carbajal said. "Rondo Craft, general manager of the El Paso and Southwestern Railroad, knew of this shipment on its way to California. For a good price, paid in gold, he agreed to tell our men how to divert it off onto a spur between Columbus and Hachita. The spur had been abandoned several years before. It was used to transport cattle from the ranch of a wealthy cattleman about three miles north of here. The spur ran through this natural cleft in the mountain where a low-producing silver and copper mine had been worked in the mid-1890's. The railroad had built a spur through to a loading pen at the ranch. The rancher eventually went bankrupt and sold out, and the spur was abandoned. This was a perfect hiding place for the train. Unfortunately we had to kill the train crew to eliminate witnesses. Fortunes of war."

"Even though they had nothing to do with the revolution," Whitlaw said grimly.

"Exactly. A dozen of our men blocked the track and leaped aboard when the train stopped, overwhelming the guards. We threw the switch and ran the train down the spur to this mountain. We then shot the crew and the guards and set off dynamite charges at both ends of this cut to cover the locomotive and cars."

"How did you take up the track so quickly?" Whitlaw asked, curious in spite of his uneasiness.

"That was the beauty of it. We didn't take it up . . . we buried it."

"You mean it's still there?"

"Ingenious, isn't it?" Carbajal grinned and blew a stream of smoke out of his nostrils.

"How did you do it in one night?"

"We planned it all in advance and it went off without a hitch. Two mules pulling a wagon containing plows and harnesses were waiting in the desert near the switch. After we ran the train into this mountain cut, we hitched a mule to each turning plow and plowed along each side of the spur, turning the soil over onto the tracks. The two plows were made differently . . . one turned the earth to the left, the other to the right. About twenty men, following with shovels, finished the job. They even dragged brush along behind to smooth out all traces of their passage."

"A powerful lot o' trouble for a load o' guns," Glasheen observed.

"At the time, we thought these guns critical to the success of the Carranza forces," Carbajal said. "We were planning to retrieve them by wagon as soon as possible, but Villa was in the way, and we were short of money because that bastard at the railroad had demanded such a stiff price, up front, for these weapons. May he rot in hell for extorting gold from our freedom fighters!"

Whitlaw could almost smell the sulphur on his breath.

"Anyway, we brought the mules back to the main line, rehitched the wagon containing the detached switch, and drove off to Mexico. The two plows are still somewhere under all this rubble.

"To the investigators, later, General Manager Craft appeared to be co-operating, but never let on that a spur had ever existed here. He even diverted the searchers toward the sidetrack that runs from Hachita to the border."

Whitlaw was still having trouble believing all this, even though he was this minute sitting atop the vanished train. "You mean the lights and the blasting and the gunfire didn't attract anyone's attention?"

"Whose?" Carbajal shrugged. "We are in the middle of nowhere. There are at least sixteen miles of desert between us and Hachita, and nearly twenty to Columbus. And this mountain did a good job muffling the sounds of explosions."

Whitlaw was already thinking that, if he were to keep his end of the agreement to help haul half this load out of here, he'd have to bring in three or four trucks by night.

As if reading his thoughts, Carbajal said: "If I still had some connection at the railroad, I might be able to uncover this spur, install a new switch, and get a locomotive to the base of this mountain. It would take a lot of digging, but these cars of rifles could be salvaged, taken to Hachita, then south to the undefended border. Of course, we would have to dispose of the bodies, then seal and repaint the cars to disguise their cargo. A lot of trouble and expense, and too many people involved." He looked directly at Whitlaw. "All wishful thinking on my part. Craft lies at the point of death from a stroke . . . that's why you are here, my friend. Here are the guns I promised, as good as the night I last saw them two years ago. It's up to the three of us to get my half loaded on some big trucks. It will take work, but it can be done with nobody the wiser."

Whitlaw hesitated. "You think the three of us are physically capable of this?"

"Absolutely. If you're having second thoughts about dealing with me, it's too late. And, if it will ease your honorable conscience, I didn't shoot the train crew and guards. Some hot-blooded soldiers did it under previous orders from Carranza himself." He stopped speaking and ground out the *cigarillo* in the grit under his boot.

A bright flash of lightning lit up the jagged slot over their heads, followed almost immediately by a crash of thunder.

"Why did you say you were the last person alive who knew about this?" Whitlaw asked.

"I kept up with the forty men who helped hide this shipment. Twenty-four were killed in a *Villista* ambush a month later, and the other sixteen have died of disease or wounds over the past two years."

"How do you know they didn't tell someone else?"

Carbajal shrugged. "They could have. But it would be like repeating a tale of lost treasure. If anyone actually believed such a story, they would not have the time or the resources to go looking for it. On the off chance that they did, do you think they could have found this? I knew exactly where to look, and even I had trouble locating it in the dark after two years. Desert shrubs have overgrown the whole area. Nature has hidden the few scars we left."

Whitlaw had to admit the Mexican was probably right. He stood up and brushed the dust off his pants. "I want to take a closer look at the cargo, and then we'd better go before this rain sets in."

Glasheen struggled to his feet, favoring both knees. He waited atop the partially buried car while the other two climbed down with the lantern to take a last look inside the boxcar. Whitlaw opened a few cases at random and saw that the shipment appeared to be undisturbed. Then they went forward to the second boxcar and, with some effort, slid back the door on one side and went in. Several cases were open and empty. "What's this?" Whitlaw asked.

"Each man involved in the raid was given a carbine and a case of ammunition as part of the spoils," Carbajal said. "This is where I got mine." He indicated the carbine that was still slung across his back.

Whitlaw lifted a carbine from a broken case and wiped off the lubricant. He worked the bolt—an extremely slick, frictionless action. A well-designed gun. He held the top of the receiver to the lantern light and read:

U.S.
Model 1896
Springfield Armory 80998

He turned it over and could make out the cartouche in the wood just abaft the trigger guard—a fancy P in a circle—the proof mark showing it had been test fired at the factory.

"I'm taking this one with me," he said. "We'll pick up a couple of cases of ammo on the way out."

Carbajal nodded. "A nice weapon. My half will still help Carranza put down Villa and the other rebel forces."

"You're going to *sell* yours to the Carranza forces? They've already paid for them once." Whitlaw smiled at the irony of it.

"Yes, but they were unable to take delivery. I will actually put the guns into their hands . . . for a considerable delivery fee. After all, the money will fund the beginning of my new life in the United States. Call it compensation for fighting and being wounded in Carranza's service."

This man can rationalize anything, Whitlaw thought.

They went back to the rear boxcar and Whitlaw handed up his carbine to Glasheen who looked relieved to have the lighted lantern close by once more. Then Whitlaw went inside and grabbed two metal ammunition boxes by the end handles and hefted them out and up to the roof of the car.

"I don't want to hire any drivers," Carbajal was saying. "The fewer who know about this, the better. Just get three trucks for the three of us. We'll work at night. I'll arrange for warehouse space just across the line in a tiny village I know of. The owner of the building owes me a favor. Once we get my half across, you can do as you wish with the rest."

As they talked, they walked along the top of the caboose to go out the way they'd come in. Whitlaw set down the metal ammo boxes and slipped out his watch, popping it open with his thumb. It was already 1:36 in the morning. He'd lost all track of time. He slid the timepiece back into his watch pocket and bent to pick up the boxes.

The desert below exploded in a roar of gunfire.

Chapter Eighteen

Thunder drowned the *pinging* of bullets off the rock walls as chips stung Whitlaw's face. He flattened himself next to the ammunition boxes. Carbajal and Glasheen scrambled to find shelter behind fallen boulders.

The thunder died away, followed by eerie silence.

"Anybody hit?" Whitlaw asked in a low voice.

"A bullet took off m'hat, but I'm as good as ever," Glasheen said.

"All right here." Carbajal's voice came from a crevice in the wall fifteen feet away.

Four more shots followed in quick succession, the slugs whining off the rocks around them. Carbajal wormed his way over to the still-burning lantern that had fallen, upright, in the shale. He closed the side shutter, blocking all but a tiny sliver of light, barely visible to the three men.

"How many, do you think?" Whitlaw asked.

"I heard at least six or seven rifles," Carbajal answered. His voice was calm, business-like.

"Let's get back inside." Whitlaw squirmed to get a grip on the ammo boxes and still keep low.

"No! Stay down and stay quiet," Carbajal whispered. "For all they know, they got the three of us with the first volley. Those second shots were just to draw our fire to see if we were still alive." Carbajal was only five yards away, but his low voice might have been issuing from the wall itself, since Whitlaw could see nothing of him.

"B'God, since I came to North America, I've taken more fire than the lads in Dublin last Sunday," Glasheen said.

"At least you're not in the hands of the British," Whitlaw grunted.

"Right you are. Whoever's out there is in no mood for takin' prisoners."

"Retreat may not be the wisest thing," Carbajal said. "I'm sure those shots came from at least two hundred yards away. If we stay still, they won't know if we're dead or wounded. And I'd bet anything they'll wait until daylight to come up and find out."

"Then what?" asked Whitlaw. "In daylight we'll just be in a worse fix, and more tired."

"We could go down under cover of darkness and pick them off, one by one," Carbajal said sarcastically, "but I wouldn't recommend it."

"It might be the law," Glasheen offered.

"No. The law long ago gave up looking for these rifles," Whitlaw said. "And if the authorities are after Carbajal, they didn't have to follow him out here. They could have arrested him right there in camp."

"I'm not wanted for anything," the Mexican said.

They heard the distant growl of an automobile or truck engine. The sound continued for about a minute, then stopped.

"So, it *was* the flash of a headlight I saw just before we came in," Whitlaw said.

"Why didn't you say something earlier?" Carbajal asked, somewhat irritated.

"Would it have made any difference? They were already on our trail and we were already here."

"So, if they have horses, they also have motor vehicles," Glasheen said.

"Just who the hell *are* they?" Whitlaw demanded. "I thought you said you were the last living person who knew the location of these rifles."

"I am. Several *Villistas* have been following me for the bounty on my head. I suspected all along they wanted me to lead them to the rifles before they sprang the trap."

"Great! Now he tells us." Whitlaw knew he should have questioned Carbajal's story much more. But it was too late for regrets.

"This small group of *Villistas* are very persistent," Carbajal went on. "For months, they've worked in relays, keeping me in sight, and some of them weren't too subtle about it."

"You're pretty nonchalant. You might at least have taken some care that you weren't followed here," Whitlaw said.

"I thought I'd given them the slip tonight," Carbajal said with no hint of apology.

"Pardon me for interrupting this debate, gentlemen," Glasheen said quietly, "but if we're going to do something, we'd best be at it. Personally I'm for retreating out the back end of this groove in the mountain."

"Good idea," Whitlaw agreed. "If those men followed you to find this place, they don't know about the cut through this mountain. So they won't have anyone stationed at the rear, waiting for us to come out the back door. We could put a lot of distance between us and them by daylight."

"Maybe . . . *if* you could find your way without stars or a compass," Carbajal said. "If they're spread out, there's a good chance you might walk right into them. Even if you got lucky, you'd still be afoot in the open desert come daylight, miles from town. And the *Villistas* who are after me always keep a half-breed Mojave tracker with them. They'd run you down in no time."

He was correct, and Whitlaw knew it. Their best chance was to fort up right here.

For several seconds, they fell silent, each man with his own thoughts.

"The rifles!" Whitlaw said suddenly. "We've got a whole arsenal right behind us. And we're in a fortified position." He turned to Carbajal in the dark. "You're the best shot. Stay here and keep watch. Glasheen and I will go back and drag a few cases of those rifles and some ammo up here." He snatched the shuttered lantern.

"Just keep as quiet as you can," Carbajal said. "These walls behind us will act as a sounding board for any noise."

Thirty seconds later, they were heaving the wooden cases to the roof of the boxcar.

"What good will all these rifles be, if only three o' us are here to shoot them?" Glasheen asked, panting, while they lugged the cases to the foot of the opening.

"We'll create a wall of fire," Whitlaw said, setting down one end of the box.

"That's the way eight of us held out for three days at the Wright ranch house," Carbajal said.

"Then get to loading these," Whitlaw ordered, shoving a metal box of ammo toward Carbajal.

He and the Irishman returned to the boxcar. "Six cases should be enough," Whitlaw said, wiping sweat from his forehead with a sleeve. "We can't manage any more than that. Grab those two boxes of ammo. I saw a few bayonets in here somewhere," he added, flashing the bull's-eye lantern around.

"Wicked stickers," Glasheen said. "Hope it doesn't

come to using those, or 'twill be our last hope."

"It's them or us," Whitlaw said grimly, forcing back the sickening image of jabbing that deadly steel into another human.

They positioned the six cases behind some rocks in the mouth of the tunnel. Thick mesquite bushes screened the opening that led down the pile of loose shale to the desert floor. Prying off the tops of the wooden cases, they proceeded to load the weapons, laying them in a row atop a table formed by the empty cases. The lantern was set in a sheltered spot with the shutter barely open, allowing just enough light to see what they were doing.

Carbajal scooped handfuls of live rounds from a metal box, flipped open the box-shaped magazine on the right side of each rifle, and dropped in five brass cartridges. Then he snapped the loading gate shut and went on to the next rifle. Every few seconds he held up a hand for silence while he listened intently. "They're closing in," he said. Apparently his senses were keener than those of the two older men. Whitlaw could detect no sound in the windless, sultry darkness.

"Do you think they'll come in the dark?" Glasheen whispered.

"*¿Quién sabe?*" The Mexican continued to load the rifles and carbines as fast as he could.

Whitlaw and Glasheen joined him; Glasheen wiped off the excess packing grease from the new guns, and Whitlaw made sure the thirty-eight rifles and carbines were laid out parallel to each other, several inches apart where they could be grabbed quickly in the very low light.

Minutes later, the task was completed. All weapons were fully loaded and cocked, with safeties on.

The explosions that had shattered the wall and partially

buried the back of the train had left several large granite boulders and about four feet of detritus atop the rail bed, blocking the entrance to the cut. Over the intervening two years, mesquite and creosote bush had taken root in the crevices and now formed a partial screen to the opening in the mountain.

Whitlaw snapped bayonets on ten of the loaded rifles, then crouched by the concealed lantern and consulted his watch. It was 2:25 a.m. He pushed the bent tin shutter of the lantern closed, leaving a tiny crack of light escaping.

Each of the three men took a weapon—Whitlaw and Carbajal, their carbines, and Glasheen, a longer rifle with bayonet attached. They settled down to wait, half sitting or lying prone on the rocky ground, several feet apart. When they spoke at all, it was in whispers.

"Wish we had a Ben-A," Glasheen whispered hoarsely.

" 'If wishes were horses, beggars would ride,' " quoted Whitlaw.

A quarter of an hour stretched out with no sound but the muttering of thunder. Perhaps the rain was skirting to the north of them.

"We'll either hear them, or they'll wait till dawn and we'll see them," Carbajal said. "Only an Apache could come up that slope with all the loose rock in total darkness and not make the least noise."

"Maybe they left while we were getting all these guns loaded," Glasheen said hopefully.

"Don't bet on it. We'd have heard them moving," Whitlaw said.

Another long stretch of silence dragged by. Except for the distant flickerings of lightning and grumblings of thunder, Whitlaw could imagine that time had come to a standstill and eternity begun. In spite of their perilous situation, he found

223

himself dozing. His head drooped forward, his cheek resting against the carbine's cool metal receiver. He fought sleepiness, but it was a losing battle. The physical exertion, the stress, the quiet darkness, his prone position, and his years all combined to drag him down to sleep.

"Whitlaw!"

His eyes flicked open at the sound of his name. "Yeah."

"They're coming," Carbajal whispered.

Whitlaw was instantly alert, the adrenaline pumping. It was still dark. How long had he dozed?

What followed was totally unexpected. Downslope, through the screen of mesquite, he saw a brief flicker of fire. Then two flaming torches were hurled high overhead, arching, to fall several feet behind them.

While the sudden light temporarily blinded them, a fusillade of rifle fire crashed and roared, the bullets ricocheting from the rocks in every direction. Whitlaw hugged the ground and thumbed off the safety of his carbine, but made no attempt to fire back. He pulled his Colt pistol and waited.

Then came the charge through the bushes, the attackers swarming up the rocky slope, slipping and sliding on the loose shale.

"Now!" Carbajal yelled.

Whitlaw aimed at the nearest moving figure. He and Glasheen emptied their fast firing Colt automatics. No time to reload. Whitlaw dropped the pistol and raised the carbine. The weapon bucked and roared. He worked the bolt action to chamber another round and fired again at the moving figures. Again and again he pulled the trigger until the five-shot magazine was empty. Dropping the hot weapon, he grabbed another. He was vaguely aware of the men on either side of him firing as fast as they could, trying to cut down the leading edge of the attacking wave. They dared not stand or kneel for a better angle of fire because of the torches back-lighting them. Individual shots came so thick and fast from both sides, the gunfire blended into one continuous roar.

An attacker escaped the rain of bullets and came for Glasheen, raising his pistol at pointblank range. The Irishman lunged upward with his empty rifle and impaled the *Villista* on the bayonet. The man fell, discharging his revolver into the ground, his weight twisting the rifle and bayonet from Glasheen's hands.

The Irishman yelled and grabbed for another loaded rifle from the pile that had been knocked from the boxes.

The blasting continued for nearly a minute longer before the attack faltered and the few remaining shadowy figures faded away down the slope. Whitlaw continued to fire at the retreating muzzle flashes until they ceased.

In the sudden silence, his ears were ringing. The inside of his mouth had a brassy taste, and he had to spit to get enough saliva working. "Everyone OK?" he croaked.

"Yeah."

The voice was so hoarse, he had to look to his left to be sure it was Glasheen.

"Carbajal?"

No answer.

"Ramón! You hurt?"

He could hear groaning below. One of the wounded attackers trying to crawl away. Whitlaw could see nothing of Carbajal in the dimness. He flipped the safety on his rifle and edged sideways toward the spot where he'd last seen the Mexican.

By the dim light of the still-flickering torches on the

ground, he found Carbajal wedged between two large rocks, carbine in hand. Whitlaw pulled him back by the shoulders, turning the limp man around to the light. He was dead. A neat, round hole in the forehead, the back of his head a bloody mass of hair.

"Shit!" Whitlaw hissed softly, lowering the body.

Glasheen crawled a few feet to them and took a look.

"They got him," Whitlaw said.

Glasheen took a deep breath. "B'God, we made 'em pay, though. There may not be any o' 'em left to collect that bounty on him."

"There won't be any reward paid if we hide his body," Whitlaw said.

Glasheen turned, listening. "I think they're goin'."

They heard the sounds of horses and the whining of a truck engine.

Whitlaw had forgotten about the weather until he was startled by a sudden flash of lightning that lit up the area with the brightness of day, followed immediately by the crack of thunder. A veil of rain swept over them. The storm had crept up and ambushed them from the backside of the mountain. The torches hissed out in the downpour. The two men took Carbajal by the shoulders and legs and rolled him into a crevice of rock near the base of the wall. Glasheen did most of the work, scooping loose shale and rocks over the body. When it was well covered, he struggled to hoist two good-size rocks and place them on top. "That should do it," he panted, opening the shutter of the lantern to inspect his work. "I didn't know y'long, but y'had your good points. God rest your soul!"

"Time to get out of this charnel house," Whitlaw said nervously, looking down into the bushes toward the inert forms of the dead attackers. "Close up that lantern . . . they might have left a sniper behind."

The two men both slung a loaded carbine on his shoulder and carried a box of ammunition while Whitlaw carried the lantern. By common consent they retreated into the cleft and climbed over the half buried train, relying on occasional flashes of lightning to show the way. Slipping and sliding, they moved past the locomotive before they dared show the lantern light to guide them the rest of the quarter mile to the end of the cut.

In a dry spot between two large boulders, they took shelter for the remaining two hours of darkness. Back to back, they kept their carbines handy, neither man able to sleep.

A gray dawn crept up over the wet desert. The storm had moved on. The men stepped carefully into the open to look around. They were on the northwest side of the mountain. After getting a good drink of rain water from a hollow in the nearby rock, they set off to hike back around the base of the mountain in the general direction of the railroad. They were careful and alert to any movement, but the desert appeared empty of humans. The *Villistas* had departed.

"I hope our wagon and team are still there," Whitlaw said, after an hour of walking. "I'm so tired, stiff, and sore. I don't relish walking all the way back to town." His right shoulder was sore from the slamming recoil of the Krags' metal butt plates.

As if to mock his words, they heard the *rattling* of the morning eastbound train in the distance, more than a mile away.

The sun had broken through the clouds and dried out their clothes. They waited until past midday to creep back up toward the site of the battle. It was deserted, and a closer inspection revealed that all the dead and wounded had been removed. In spite of the rain, traces of blood still lingered on the rocks here and there, and the mesquite was mashed down in spots. Brass cartridge cases twinkled in the sunlight. Their wagon and span of mules were gone.

"We'd best get to walking, if we're to get home by dark," Glasheen said. "These wet boots o' mine are beginnin' to wear a blister."

"Might as well leave this ammo box," Whitlaw said, opening it and scooping a handful of cartridges into his pocket. Before setting off, they lightened their load a little further by stacking the gun belts with the empty Colts in the rocks. Then they started their trek across the desert toward Columbus.

Whitlaw plodded along, head down, his mind and legs both heavy from lack of sleep.

He'd never been in the military, never fired a shot in anger or self-defense. Yet, beginning with the raid on Columbus, slightly over a month ago, he'd been caught up in at least five gun battles. The odds of his surviving any more of this were rapidly diminishing. Even during the strafing, he'd been attempting to save other lives besides his own. "Greater love than this, no man has. . . ." In the heat of each fight, his survival instinct had taken over. Still, his stomach was queasy with a vague sense of guilt. He'd never even hunted deer or pheasant. And now this—gunning down other human beings. War and murder had existed in the world since Cain and Abel, but that didn't mean he had to be part of it. There was a commandment against such things.

He spat a foul taste from his mouth and took a swig from the canteen.

A half hour later, Glasheen sank down wearily in his

tracks. "B'God, I'm beginning to feel like a beggar."

"What?" Whitlaw shuffled to a halt.

Glasheen pointed. In the distance stood their mule team, still hitched to the wagon. "As you told me last night . . . 'If wishes were horses, beggars would ride.' "

Chapter Nineteen

"I hate to see you go," Whitlaw said, gripping Glasheen's hand three weeks later as they stood in the bright sunshine of the Columbus depot platform. "I feel I've known you all my life."

"It's sad I am t'be leavin'," the Irishman concurred. "You've put a number of these gray hairs in m'head, but I wouldn't have missed it for anything, even though a couple of times I didn't think I would ever see m'Annie again. I've felt more alive these two months past than I have in years."

"Why don't you send the rifles on ahead, and stay for a time?"

Glasheen grinned. "I'd be bored. You've given me a taste for adventure, and things have gotten dull around here." He picked up his small canvas grip. "I'll travel on the freighter, from Galveston, with the guns."

"Those Krags weren't free. Tell me, did the insurance company give you a good deal on the whole shipment?" Whitlaw asked, falling in beside him as they walked toward the train chugging to a stop in a *hiss* of escaping steam.

"Let's say, I levered 'em down to m'price."

"Your Celtic charm," Whitlaw said. "And I got what I wanted by clearing my name. A Union Pacific official gave a sort of grudging apology to a reporter for the UPI."

"The general manager of the El Paso and Southwestern

was exposed as the crook. Too bad he didn't live to stand trial."

"No matter. He's already reported to a higher court," Whitlaw said. "As I keep telling you, things always work out for the best."

Glasheen set his bag by the steps of the passenger coach. "A man like you depends entirely too much on the providence o' the Almighty."

"I didn't know that was possible." Whitlaw smiled.

"Well, take good care o' Maud Wright and her daughter," Glasheen said, wringing Whitlaw's hand and taking up his grip.

"She won't need much looking after. She's been hired on at the hotel, and plans to rent our old adobe place after I move."

"Move?"

"Back to Iowa for now. To be near the grandkids. My son wants me to write down an account of all my adventures. I might even take up flying again."

Glasheen rolled his eyes, then stepped up into the coach. He turned back. "Donahue sent word o' the place where they've settled Annie. This is the address." He handed Whitlaw a slip of paper. "Write me when ye get moved."

"I'll do better than that. Tell your wife I'll be over for a visit in the fall."

A wide grin split Glasheen's face. The steam whistle blasted and the train jerked into motion. "B'God, I'll keep a good head on the Guinness!"

Epilogue

Pancho Villa was never caught. During a battle with rival revolutionaries, he was shot from behind by one of his own soldiers, a Mexican peasant Villa had forcibly recruited. Suffering from a serious leg wound, he was carried deep into Mexico by his followers who cared for him until he recovered and eventually emerged several months later, bold and brutal as ever.

Pancho Villa and Emiliano Zapata remained Carranza's main rivals for power, until Zapata was assassinated April 10, 1919. Villa fought on, even raiding Carranza forces in Juárez, across the Río Grande from El Paso, on June 14, 1919. Stray bullets were hitting and killing residents in El Paso, until General James Irwin ordered artillery to shell a concentration of *Villistas* near the Juarez racetrack, then sent Colonel Tompkins with a troop of cavalry across the river to attack and drive off Villa and his men.

One of Carranza's supporters, Alvaro Obregón, persuaded his own troops to turn on Carranza and drive him from power. Carranza was caught and killed while fleeing toward Veracruz with most of the contents of the treasury.

Two months later, Villa decided to quit the fight and surrender to the government in return for a house and land and fifty of his soldiers as bodyguards. He lived peacefully on his 25,000-acre *hacienda* for three years. But he had made many enemies. On July 20, 1923, he and five body-guards were gunned down by eight men as he drove down a Parral street in his Dodge touring car. A sixth bodyguard, Ramón Contreras, although wounded, escaped the ambush.

Villa now lies headless in his grave. In a morbid twist of fate, his corpse was dug up and decapitated a year or two later. No one knows why. One rumor has it that Ramón Contreras, the surviving bodyguard, was trying to collect a reward of $1,000 that he mistakenly thought American officials had posted for Villa's head.

General Pershing and all his American troops were finally recalled to the United States in January, 1917. A much bigger war awaited them on the continent of Europe.

A partition of Ireland in the 1920s did not bring peace to the country. In a continuing effort to reunite Ireland, guerrilla warfare against British protection of the northern counties goes on to this day.

About the Author

Tim Champlin, born John Michael Champlin in Fargo, North Dakota, was graduated from Middle Tennessee State University and earned a Master's degree from Peabody College in Nashville, Tennessee. Beginning his career as an author of the Western story with SUMMER OF THE SIOUX in 1982, the American West represents for him "a huge, ever-changing block of space and time in which an individual had more freedom than the average person has today. For those brave, and sometimes desperate souls who ventured West looking for a better life, it must have been an exciting time to be alive." Champlin has achieved a notable stature in being able to capture that time in complex, often exciting, and historically accurate fictional narratives. He is the author of two series of Western novels, one concerned with Matt Tierney who comes of age in SUMMER OF THE SIOUX and who begins his professional career as a reporter for the Chicago *Times-Herald* covering an expeditionary force venturing into the Big Horn country and the Yellowstone, and one with Jay McGraw, a callow youth who is plunged into outlawry at the beginning of COLT LIGHTNING. There are six books in the Matt Tierney series and with DEADLY SEASON a fifth featuring Jay McGraw. In THE LAST CAMPAIGN, Champlin provides a compelling narrative of Geronimo's last days as a renegade leader. SWIFT THUNDER is an exciting and compelling story of the Pony Express. WAYFARING STRANGERS is an extraordinary story of the California Gold Rush. In all of Champlin's stories there are always unconventional plot ingredients, striking historical details, vivid characterizations of the multitude of ethnic and cultural diversity found on the frontier, and narratives rich and original and surprising. His exuberant tapestries include lumber schooners sailing the West Coast, early-day wet-plate photography, daredevils who thrill crowds with gas balloons and the first parachutes, tong wars in San Francisco's Chinatown, Basque sheepherders, and the *Penitentes* of the Southwest, and are always highly entertaining. FIRE BELL IN THE NIGHT is his next **Five Star Western**.